Eliza Margaret Gollan

The Mystery of a Turkish Bath

Eliza Margaret Gollan

The Mystery of a Turkish Bath

ISBN/EAN: 9783743317444

Manufactured in Europe, USA, Canada, Australia, Japa

Cover: Foto ©Andreas Hilbeck / pixelio.de

Manufactured and distributed by brebook publishing software
(www.brebook.com)

Eliza Margaret Gollan

The Mystery of a Turkish Bath

THE MYSTERY

OF A

TURKISH BATH

BY

"RITA,"

AUTHOR OF "DAME BURDEN," "LIKE DIAN'S KISS," "A SINLESS SECRET," ETC., ETC.

——— ———

NEW YORK
JOHN W. LOVELL COMPANY
150 WORTH STREET, CORNER MISSION PLACE

CONTENTS

— ◆ —

THE MYSTERY OF A TURKISH BATH.

CHAPTER I.

THE FIRST ROOM.

"I TAKE them for rheumatic gout," said a slight, dark-haired woman to her neighbour, as she leant back in a low lounging-chair, and sipped some water an attendant had just brought her. "You would not suppose I suffered from such a complaint, would you?" —and she held up a small arched foot, with a scarcely perceptible swelling in the larger joint. She laughed somewhat affectedly, and the neighbour, who was fat and coarse, and had decided gouty symptoms herself, looked at her with something of the contempt an invalid elephant might be supposed to bestow on a buzzing fly.

"You made that remark the last time you were here," she said; "and I told you, if you suffered from a suppressed form of the disease, it would be all the worse for you. Much better for it to come out—my doctor says."

There was no doubt about the disease having "come out" in the person of the speaker. It had " come out " in her face, which was brilliantly rubicund ; in her hands, and ankles and feet, which were a distressful spectacle of " knobs " and " bumps " of an exaggerated phrenological type—perhaps also in her temper, which was fierce and fiery as her complexion, as most of the frequenters of the Baths knew, and the attendants also, to their cost.

The small, dark lady, with the arched feet, lapsed into sulky silence, and let her eyes wander over the room to see if anyone she knew was there.

The Baths were of an extensive and sumptuous description — fitted up with almost oriental luxury and comfort, and attached to a monster hotel, built by an enterprising Company of speculators, at an English winter resort, in H——shire.

The Company had proudly hoped that lavish expenditure, a beautiful situation, and the disinterested recommendation of fashionable physicians, would induce English people to discover that there were spots and places in their own land as healthy and convenient as Auvergne, or Wiesbaden, or the Riviera. But though the coast views were fine, and the scenery picturesque, and the monster hotel itself stood on a commanding eminence, surrounded by darkly-beautiful pine woods, and was fitted up with every luxury of modern civilization, including every specimen of Bath that human ingenuity had devised, the Company looked blankly at the returns on their balance-sheet, and one or two Directors murmured audible complaints at special Board meetings, against the fashion-able physicians who had not acted up to their promises, or proved deserving of the sub-stantial bonus which had been more than hinted at, as a reward for recommended patients.

On this December morning, some half-dozen ladies, of various ages and stability of person, and all suffering, in a greater or less degree, from various fashionable complaints —such as neuralgia, indigestion, rheumatism, or its aristocratic cousin, rheumatic-gout— were in Room No. I. of the Turkish Bath.

The female form is generally supposed to be " divine," and poets and painters have, from time immemorial, rhapsodized over " beauty unadorned." It is probable that such poets and painters have never been gratified by such a vision of feminine charms as Room No. I. presented.

Light and airy garments were, certainly, to be seen, but not—forms. It was, of course, a question of taste, as to whether the fat women, or the thin women, looked the worst —probably the former, if one might judge by the two samples of the lady who had arched feet, and the lady who had *not.*

Both were staying at the hotel, and were respectively named — Mrs. Masterman, and Mrs. Ray Jefferson. Mrs. Masterman was a widow. Mrs. Ray Jefferson had a husband. He was an American, blessed with many dollars, amassed on the strength of an " Invention." When Mr. Jefferson spoke of the Invention, people usually supposed it to be of a mechanical nature. As they became more familiar with him, they learnt that it was something "Chemical." No one quite knew what, but it became associate l in their minds with "vats" and "boilers," and large works somewhere "down Boston way." There could be no doubt of the excellence of the Invention, because Mr. Ray Jefferson said it was known, and used all over Eu-rope, and its success was backed by dollars to an apparently unlimited extent. The Inventor and his wife had sumptuous rooms, but they were not averse to mixing with their "fellow-man," or rather "woman," —for Mrs. Jefferson rejoiced in the possession of certain Parisian *toilettes*, and was not selfish enough to keep them only for the eyes of her lord and master.

She was grudgingly but universally acknowledged to be the best-dressed woman in the hotel—except, of course, when she was in the Turkish Baths, which unfortunately reduced its fequenters to one level of apparelling, a garment which made up in simplicity for any lack of elegance.

The shape was always the same—viz., short in the skirt, low in the neck, and bare as to sleeves. The material was generally pink cotton, or white with a red border.

Mrs. Jefferson was quite American enough to have "notions" on dress, more or less original and extravagant. Finding her companion was unusually silent this morning, she gave up her thoughts to the devising of a special toilet for the Bath.

These garments were so hideous, she told herself, that it was no wonder people looked such guys in them. Still there was no reason why she should not have something *chic* and novel for herself—something which should arouse the envy of, and make the wearer appear quite different to, the other women.

The choice of style was easy enough—something Grecian and artistic—but the material discomposed her. It was hardly possible to have a bath of this description without one's garment getting into a moist and clinging condition—leaving alone the after processes of shampooing, *douche*, and plunge. So silk, or satin, or woollen material was out of the question, and cotton was common, not to say vulgar.

She knitted her brows with a vigour demanded by so absorbing a subject: the white head-cloth fell off, and she felt that her fringe was all out of curl and lay straight on her forehead in most unbecoming fashion. That also would have to be considered in the question of costume—a head-dress which should combine use and ornament. The idea of having only a wet, white rag on one's head! No wonder people looked "objects!" Perhaps it would be better to coil the hair about the brow and have no fringe, or at least only a few loose locks that would look equally well, straight or curled.

As Mrs. Ray Jefferson was taking all this trouble about her personal appearance, when that appearance would only gratify the sight of a few members of her own sex who were generally too much taken up with their own ailments or complaints to care what their fellow-sufferers looked like, it shows the fallacy of a popular superstition that women only care to dress for men. Believe me, no—they dress for critics, the critics of their own sex, who with one contemptuous glance can sweep a *toilette* into insignificance, and make its wearer miserable, or, by some envious approbation, are reluctantly compelled to bestow on it the seal of success

Is it for men, think you, that those delicate *nuances* and tints and shades are harmonized and put together? Such a conceit is only pardonable in a set of beings who possess not the delicate faculty of " detail," and who, with a limited knowledge of even cardinal colours, describe the graces and beauties of a *toilette* by saying the wearer had on something white, or something black, or something red, but " it suited her down to the ground." A few misguided individuals have even been known to take refuge in the remark (made historic now by comic papers) that " they never look *under* the table," when asked what certain ladies had on. But this is trifling, and only applicable to dinner parties.

Mrs. Ray Jefferson's thoughts had not prevented her from taking stock of the other inmates of the room. One or two were lying on couches, but most of them seemed to prefer the low comfortable chairs, that were like rocking-chairs without the rockers.

No one spoke. They looked solemn and suffering, and appeared intent merely on the symptoms of distilled moisture on the visible portion of their persons.

" I think," said Mrs Jefferson, " I shall go into the second room. I can stand some more heat."

She made the remark, abstractedly, in the direction of her neighbour, who only looked at her in a bored and ill-tempered fashion, as befitted one who had gout without arched feet to display as compensation.

"You and I are the only hotel people here," went on Mrs. Jefferson, as she took up the glass of water and the head-cloth preparatory to moving away. Then she laughed again as she looked at her companion's flushed countenance and generally distressed appearance. "What a comfort," she said, "that we won't look quite such objects at dinner-time! I always find a bath improves my complexion, don't you?"

Mrs. Markham gave an impatient grunt. "As if it mattered what one looks like in a bath!" she said. "Do you Americans live in public all your lives? You seem to be always thinking of your clothes, or your looks!"

Mrs. Jefferson opened her lips to reply with suitable indignation, but the words were cut short by a gasp of astonishment, and lost themselves in one wondering, long-drawn monosyllable—"My——!"

The gouty sufferer also looked up, and in the direction of the doorway, and though she said nothing, her eyes expressed as much surprise as was compatible with a sluggish temperament, and a disposition to cavil at most things and persons that were presented to her notice.

The object on which the two pair of feminine eyes rested was only the figure of a woman standing between the thick oriental curtains that partitioned off the dressing from the shampooing and douche rooms.

A woman—but a woman so beautiful that she held even her own sex dumb with admiration. She was tall, but not too tall for perfect grace ; and slender, but with the slenderness of some young pictured goddess. She was dark, too, but with a pale clear skin that was more lovely than any dead blonde whiteness ; and to crown her charms, she had long rippling hair of jet black hue that was parted from her brow and fell like a veil to her delicate arched feet, and through which the serious, darkly - glowing eyes looked straight at the wondering faces before her.

The pause she made before entering was brief, but not so brief that every eye there had not scanned enviously and wonderingly her perfect beauty—from the clear-cut, exquisite face and bare, beautifully - shaped arms, to the graceful ankles, gleaming white as sculptured marble through the veiling hair.

Mrs. Jefferson first recovered speech.

"Who is she?" she whispered eagerly. "Not at our hotel I think. Looks like a walking advertisement of a new hair restorer. She'd be a fortune to them if she'd have her photograph taken so !"

The new comer meanwhile advanced and took one of the chairs near Mrs. Jefferson. That lady suffered strongly from the curiosity that is characteristic of her admirable nation. She re-seated herself for the purpose of studying the strange vision, and, not being in the least degree afflicted with English reticence, she set the ball of conversation going by an immediate remark :

"Had any of these baths before ? "

The person addressed looked at her with grave and serious eyes.

" No," she said ; and her voice was singularly clear and sweet, but with something foreign in the slow accentuation of words. "I only arrived at this hotel last night."

" Oh ! " said Mrs. Jefferson, " is that so ? I thought I hadn't seen you before. Come for your health ? "

" Yes," said the stranger, accepting a glass of water from the attendant, who had just come forward.

" Not gout, I suppose ? " suggested Mrs. Jefferson, conscious that there were arched feet in the world even more exquisite in shape and size than her own.

"Gout! Oh, no ! " said the stranger, smiling faintly. "They say my nerves are not strong. I sleep badly, I am easily startled, and easily fatigued." She paused a moment, and one delicate hand, glittering with rings, pushed back the dark weight of rippling hair from her brow. " I have had a great mental shock," she said, quietly. "Such things require time . . . one cannot easily forget . . ."

Her eyes had grown dreamy and abstracted. The hand that had pushed back her heavy hair fell on her lap. She looked at it and its shining rings, and Mrs. Jefferson's sharp glance followed hers. Was there a plain gold circlet among that glittering array ?— was the beautiful stranger wife or maiden ?

"If any man saw her now!" she thought involuntarily. "My——! I would'nt give much for his peace of mind afterwards! What owls she makes us all look!"

"Nerves are queer things," she said aloud. "Can't say I'm much troubled with them, except here," and she moved her foot explanatorily. "Just that joint. It's agony sometimes. Suppressed gout, you know. You wouldn't think so to look at it, would you?"

"That the gout was—suppressed? certainly I should," answered the stranger, smiling. "There is no external sign of it. I always thought gout meant large lumps, and swellings of the joints."

"So it does," said Mrs. Jefferson, with an involuntary glance at the moist and crimson sufferer on her right. "But *my* form of it is different. It is much worse, but no one sympathises with me because it doesn't *look* so bad as the other gout."

"It is not often that people do sympathise with illness," said the beautiful woman. "When we ourselves are well, we think suffering can't be so very great after all, and when we are ill we are quite sure no one else has to bear so much pain. Human nature is essentially selfish. It is a natural incident of living at all that we should estimate our own life as more important than our neighbours.'"

"Well," laughed Mrs. Jefferson, "if we sacrificed it to them, it might be a doubtful benefit. I often thank my stars I wasn't born in the age of martyrs. If I had been, I'm sure the very sight of the rack or the faggot would have made me swear anything."

"The history of religions is a very curious history," said the stranger in her low clear tones. "Looked at dispassionately, it has done very little for mankind in general, save to prove one fundamental truth that is more significant than any doctrine or dogma. That truth is the inherent need in all humanity of something to worship From the highest to the lowest degrees of civilization that need has made itself the exponent of external forms. It is the kernel of all religions."

"A kernel that is surrounded with a very hard shell," said Mrs. Jefferson glibly. She liked discussions, and was accustomed to say she could talk on any subject—having indeed come from a country where women did talk on any subject, whether they were acquainted. with it or not. "I don't think there is much spirituality in any modern religion," she went on. "I surmise it's dead. Science has got the upper hand of theology and means to keep it. People are not content now-a-days with being told 'you must believe so and so.' They want a reason for believing. You're not a Romanist, are you?" she added suddenly.

"I—oh no," said the stranger with a faint smile.

"I'm glad of that, for I was just going to say that the Church of Rome has done more to retard rational and spiritual progress than any other. I don't believe in the voice of man barring the way to inquiry. God made man, and, as far as I have ever been able to learn, He made them all on one pattern. The offices and dignities they give themselves won't make them one whit greater or more important in His eyes."

"You are a democrat, I see," said the beautiful woman, looking gravely and scrutinizingly at the eager flushed face, with its ruffled damp curls, and quick restless eyes.

"Well," said Mrs. Jefferson, "I don't exactly know what I am. My views are liberal on most subjects. I've travelled a good bit, and I think that enlarges the mind I've just run over to have a look at England. Our people are laughing at her pretty well The Gladstone party have made a lovely hash of affairs haven't they? But perhaps you don't care for politics, being foreign."

"Oh, yes, I do," answered her strange companion. "And I am specially interested in English politics," she added. "Like yourself I was curious to see a nation who seemed determined to court their own shame, and to deify the being whose career is signally marked by obloquy and disaster."

"His day is pretty well over, I fancy," said Mrs. Jefferson, eagerly scenting an opportunity for a brilliant display of political knowledge " That Irish business has settled him. They call him the greatest statesman of the age! A man at dinner last night was lauding him up to the skies. There was quite a battle about him. We showed, however, that, putting his talking powers aside, he really is no statesman —only a grasping selfish old bungler, who cares nothing for his country except it keeps him in office, and has done nothing really great or good during his whole career. They make a fuss about the Education Act, but the credit of passing that belongs to Foster. As for the Disestablishment of the Irish Church, that is a disgraceful business—a robbery of the dead who had left their money to support a faith they believed in. He is responsible—to my thinking—for all the anarchy, confusion and misery in that poor unhappy Ireland. I believe," and she leant forward and dropped her voice, " I believe that at heart the man is more than half a Romanist. See how he has favoured the High Church party, and if ever he gives a clerical appointment it is always to a Ritualist priest. They don't call themselves *clergymen* now. Well,—" and she drew herself up once more, "I, for one, wouldn't like to have his sins on my shoulders. I should think he ought to be haunted by as many victims as Napoleon Buonaparte. What with financial humbug, war taxes—the blunders of the Alabama business—the disgrace and bloodshed of the Transvaal affair and the Egyptian war—crowned by the undying and never to be forgotten shame of Gordon's sacrificed life, I wonder he can lay down his head at night and sleep. When he heard of that hero Gordon's death he should have taken a pistol and blown out his blundering brains But perhaps," she added more calmly, " he was afraid of meeting his victims until he couldn't help himself. However, he might have gone into one of those 'retreats' his favourite Ritualists are so fond of, and spared England any more blunders and follies."

" You are very bitter against him," said the stranger calmly. " Be sure that his own actions will also be his own avengers. Life would be made much more tolerable if we would only keep that fact before us. To my mind there is no backbone or support in a religion that teaches irresponsibility. That is the great fault of you Christians. Your faith is not a thing you take hold of, and grasp and act upon. Hence your many national disasters. You shelve your future, or what you call your salvation, on the merits of a Sacrifice, and think yourselves relieved of all further trouble. In the world, and in society, religion is a tabooed subject—it is only kept for Sundays and for churches. I believe your clergy know no more of the *real* doctrines of Christianity, those deep and *mystical* truths underlying the teachings of Christ, than the child at his mother's knee. I have been to your great cathedrals and churches. I saw only lip-service and routine. I heard only stale maxims, weak explanations of the allegories and parables that fill your Biblical records; flowing rhetoric and vague expressions of some undefinable joy and glory in an equally undefinable Hereafter, that was sometimes described as a place, and sometimes as a state. That was all. I feel such things cannot long stand against the tide of advancing thought. Modern Christianity is not the Sermon on the Mount, and has little title to the name of its founder. It has not a feather's weight of importance in the minds of the worldly, the fashionable, the pleasure-seeking : its sentiment is extinct, save in a few faithful ignorant hearts, who adore what they cannot comprehend, and live in a state of hope that all will come right in some vague future."

The beautiful eyes had grown sad and thoughtful. They rested on the eager wondering face before her, yet seemed to look through and beyond it, as the eyes of one who sees a vision that is mere airy nothingness to the surrounding crowd.

"It will come right," she went on slowly and dreamily, "but not as men think, and not because the religion of earth teaches fear of punishment and hope of reward as the basis of spiritual faith. No. Something higher and holier and deeper than any motive of self-safety will perfect what is best in man and eliminate what is vile."

"If that is so," interposed Mrs. Jefferson, glibly, as she rose from her chair to proceed to the Second Room—"I guess man will want a pretty long time to 'perfect' in. I don't see how he's going to do it here."

"I did not say 'here,'" answered the stranger, in her slow, calm way, as she, too, rose and prepared to follow the little American. "For what, think you, are the ages of Eternity intended?—sleep and dreams?"

Mrs. Jefferson gave a little shudder "I surmise we're getting a little too deep," she said. "Let's keep to Gladstone and the Irish Question while the thermometer's at 110."

CHAPTER II.

THE SECOND ROOM.

THE second room differed in no way from the first, except in the matter of heat.

The beautiful stranger floated in—her face

all the lovelier for the faint rosy flush that glowed through the clear skin. If Mrs. Ray Jefferson's admiration was envious, at least it was genuine. She had never really believed in perfect feminine beauty before—beauty that shone supreme without the aid of dress and frippery—but here it was—a glowing and palpable fact. The simple white drapery with its border of scarlet floated with the grace of its own perfect simplicity around that perfect form, and never was royal mantle more splendid than the rippling hair that crowned her head and fell in its luxuriance of curls and waves to her feet. As they again seated themselves side by side, Mrs Jefferson remembered that she was not yet acquainted with the nationality of the stranger. She hastened to repair the error of such ignorance.

"You speak English wonderfully for a foreigner," she said; "it would puzzle anyone to make out where *you* were raised—Russian, I surmise?"

"No," said the stranger, quietly, "though I have lived there a great deal. It was my husband's country."

Mrs. Jefferson looked radiant. She was married, then. That was something to have learnt. "*Was*"—she said quickly, "Is he not living then?"

"No." The beautiful face grew a shade paler. "I would rather not talk about it," she said. "His death was very tragic and terrible"

"I'm sorry," said the little American, with ready contrition; "don't think I'm curious," she added, suddenly. "but one doesn't see woman like you every day. I surmise you'll make a sensation in the hotel."

"I have my own private rooms here," was the quiet response. "I shall not mix with the other visitors."

"Oh," cried Mrs. Jefferson, her face clouding, "I call that cruel. There are really some very good people here—titles, if you like them—money, if you care for that—one or two geniuses—a musician and a poet who are working for a future generation, because they can't get appreciated here—and the usual crowd of mediocrities. Oh, you really must come to our evenings; they'd amuse you immensely. We're quite dependent on ourselves for society. This is the dullest of dull holes, still we manage to get a bit spry now and then. Now, you—why, if you'd only show yourself to be looked at, you'd be doing the whole hotel a good turn."

The stranger shook her head. "Society never amuses me," she said. "It has nothing to offer that can rival the charms of books, art, and solitude. I possess all three."

Mrs. Jefferson opened her eyes wide. "The first and the last," she said, "are comprehensible as travelling companions, but what about the middle one?"

"In my train I have a blind musician, whose equal I have never met, and a boy sculptor whose genius will one day astonish the world. For myself, I paint and I write, and I have a store of books that will outlast the longest limit of companionship. Can you tell me what better things the world will give?"

Mrs. Ray Jefferson murmured something

vaguely about amusement and distraction. She was growing more and more perplexed about this beautiful Mystery. Anyone who travelled about with a train of attendants must surely be a princess at the very least.

"Amusement!"—the stranger smiled. "Does society ever *really* give us that? We have to smile when we are bored—to tell polite falsehoods every hour—to eat and drink when we would rather fast—to awake all sorts of evil passions in other people's minds if we are better-looking or better dressed, or more admired; and have them aroused in our own if we are *not?* Does a ball amuse? Does a dinner-party? Does even a comedy, after the first quarter of an hour? I can answer for myself in the negative, at all events."

"Gracious!" exclaimed Mrs. Jefferson wonderingly. "You must be a strange person, and you look so young. Why, I should have thought you were just the age for society? Don't you care to be admired?"

"Not in the least. I have learnt the value of men's passions. A quiet life is more wholesome and infinitely more contenting than anything society can offer."

"For a time, perhaps; but it would become dull and monotonous, I should think."

"Never, if you have the mind to appreciate it. The companionship I value will always come to me. I do not need to seek it in the world."

"You are fortunate," said Mrs. Jefferson, somewhat sarcastically. "Ordinary mortals have to take what they can get. Still, I suppose such things are only a matter of personal

disposition. If one has the mood for enjoyment, one can find it anywhere; if not—well,
a funeral or a comedy would be equally
amusing."

"I suppose," said the stranger, quietly,
"you have the mood."

"Well, I'm blessed with a pretty fair
capacity for enjoying all that comes in my
way," said the little American, frankly. "I
like studying human nature, even though I'm
not clever enough to describe it. It's like the
critics, you know, who find it so powerful
easy to cut up a book, yet couldn't write one
themselves to save their lives. Phew—w!
how hot it is here! How do you contrive to
look so cool?"

"I can stand a great deal of heat," answered
the other, tranquilly. "I have Eastern blood
in my veins, on my mother's side. Is that the
hottest room?" she added, nodding in the
direction of the third doorway.

"Yes. I suppose you won't go there?
I never dare put my nose inside. It's enough
to scorch the skin off you."

"I don't suppose it can be hotter than the
rooms in the East," answered the stranger, as
she rose and moved towards it. She stood for
a moment looking in, then turned back and
smiled at her late companion. "Oh, I can
bear it," she said, and disappeared from sight.

The little American pouted and looked disturbed. "What a shame! I had ever so
many more things to ask her," she said, "and
to think, after all, I don't know her name, or
even to what country she belongs, and I did
so want the whole story pat for the *table-d'hôte*

dinner to-night. . . . 'Ready to be shampooed?—oh, yes, Morrison; I'm just about 'done through'; I'm glad you can take me first."

She rose abruptly and followed the attendant past the flushed and perspiring groups who were still comparing notes as to different ailments and degrees of moisture, occasionally holding out their arms for mutual inspection.

"I wonder," she said to herself, "how that one woman manages to look so different. Why, we get uglier and uglier, and she only more and more beautiful. Perhaps she's a Rosicrucian!"

*   *   *   *   *

CHAPTER III.

THE COOLING ROOM.

A LONG room, down the centre of which ran a row of couches; on either side were the dressing-rooms, curtained off from the main apartment by curtains of dark Oriental blue, bordered with dull red. In the large bay window stood the dressing-tables and mirrors.

Mrs. Ray Jefferson had it all to herself, as, wrapped in an enormous sheet of Turkish towelling, she emerged from the processes of shampooing and douche. She laid herself down on one of the couches, and the attendant, Morrison, threw another Turkish wrap over her, and left her to the enjoyment of the coffee she had ordered, and which was placed on one of the numerous small tables scattered about.

According to all rules of the baths, she

should have rested calmly and patiently on that couch, until such time as she was cool enough to don her ordinary attire, but the little American, was of a restless and impatient disposition, and of all things hated to be inactive.

The attendant had scarcely left the room before she raised herself to a sitting position, and took a survey of her appearance in one of the mirrors. It did not appear to be very satisfactory. She turned abruptly away and reached some magazines from an adjoining table. Armed with these she once more sought her couch, and after tossing two or three contemptuously aside, she at last seemed to find one periodical that interested her. She grew so absorbed in its contents, that she scarcely heard the entrance of the beautiful woman who had so interested her, and who now took the next couch to her own, and lay down in an attitude of indolent grace that was quite in keeping with her appearance.

"You seem interested," she remarked, as she glanced at the absorbed face of her neighbour.

Mrs. Jefferson looked up sharply. "Well," she said, turning the magazine round to read its title. "This is about the queerest story I ever read. I wish people wouldn't write improbabilities that no one *can* swallow."

"The question is rather what is an improbability?" answered her companion. "It is only a matter of the capacity of the age to receive what is new. A few years ago electricity was improbable, yet look at the telegraph and the telephone. Still further back, who would have believed that railways would exist above ground and under ground, and mock at the difficulties of rivers and moun. tains? What have you discovered strange enough to be called 'improbable'?"

"Oh! it's a story of a man who gets out of his own body and does all sorts of queer things, and then goes back to it again, just when he pleases. Finally, he falls in love with a woman as queer as himself, and finding he has a rival, he just gets rid of him by force of will-power. However, the day they are to be married, the woman is found dead in her bed. It appears that she also could get out of her body when she felt inclined, but she did it once too often, and could'nt get back in time, so they buried her, at least they buried one of her bodies; as far as I can make out she had *two*."

"And you think that improbable?" questioned the stranger calmly.

Her beautiful deep eyes were looking straight into the flushed excited face beside her. Mrs. Ray Jefferson met their gaze, and was conscious of an odd little unaccountable thrill.

"Certainly I do," she said. "Who could believe that anyone can jump in or out of their skin just as the fancy takes them?"

The stranger's beautiful lips grew scornful. "Oh!" she said, "if you like to put the subject in that light, it may well look ridiculous and impossible. Ignorance is always more or less arrogant. It is man's habit to fancy that all creation was made for him. There are few things of which he is so utterly ignorant, and of which he thinks so little, as that mystery of *himself* incarnated in the temporary prison-house of flesh and blood. Did he once realise what he might be—did he ever raise his eyes from the glow-worm light of earth to the stupendous glories of the sun of wisdom, he would know better than to cavil at what you call 'improbable.' For in nature all things are possible, but man has neither time nor patience to trace out their mysteries, or seek in their development the key to those mysteries."

"Gracious sakes," muttered Mrs. Jefferson to herself in alarm. "I'm sure she's a Rosicrucian or something of that sort. It's interesting, but uncanny. I'm quite out of my depth. I don't know what she means. Do you really mean to say," she added aloud, "that this story might be true; that you have two bodies and can slip from one to the other?"

A dark frown crept over the beautiful face. "You talk as foolishly as a child," she said with contempt. You know nothing of the subject you are discussing, therefore anything I might say would sound incomprehensible. The grossness of the flesh stifles and kills the subtle workings of the spirit. To you life is only a pleasure ground, and the more your own personal satisfaction is obtainable, the more you cling to its spurious enjoyments. If you once cut yourself adrift from such follies, your eyes would be opened, your senses quickened, and you would recognise possibilities and marvels that now are no more to you than sunlight to the blind worm that burrows in the ground." She stretched out her hand and took the book from the passive hand of her astounded companion, and glanced rapidly over its pages.

"'Light in Darkness.' Ah, truly it is needed," she said, her eyes kindling, her face glowing, until her beauty seemed more than mortal. "But we shall never reach it till we learn to master the senses, to cut the chains of worldly prejudice and conventionalism. They are bold teachers, these," and she tossed the magazine back to the still silent critic of its contents. "You would do well," she said, "to make yourself acquainted with some of these subjects. I think you would find them more interesting than ball-rooms and Paris toilettes."

Mrs. Jefferson recovered her tongue at that slight to her beloved vanities.

"Tastes differ," she said coolly. "I'm very well content with the world as it is and with myself as I am. I don't believe any good ever comes of prying into subjects we're not intended to know anything about."

"I might ask you," said the stranger, with visible contempt, "how you are so surely convinced of what we are intended to know, and what not? There is no hard and fast rule laid down for us that I am aware of."

"Oh!" stammered Mrs. Jefferson, with some confusion, "I'm sure the Bible says that somewhere. 'Thus far shalt thou go and no further,' you know. It is arrogant to attempt to penetrate the mysteries of the other world. When we go there we shall know them soon enough."

"How glibly you nineteenth - century Christians talk of the 'other world,'" cried the beautiful woman, with contempt. She tossed back the weight of her rich hair and sat up, looking like an inspired prophetess. "Yet you acknowledge you know nothing of it. Your priests cannot explain it, so they take refuge in the plea that inquiry is presumptuous. Science cannot explain it; Reason falters at the threshold before the stumbling - block of its long - cherished ignorance whose only legacy has been Fear. And it is all because you live in falsehood —because you are false to your *inner* life, and think only of the outer; because you are all in chains of superstition—of worldly bondage, of family prejudices, and, above all, of self-delusion."

"Have you come to preach to us, then?" asked the little American superciliously "There is little use in decrying a private or national disease unless you are provided with a remedy."

"If an angel from Heaven came down to preach you would not believe!" said the stranger, growing suddenly calm as she sank back on her pillow. "No, I have no mission. I am only one who has looked out on life and learnt its bitter truths, and seen its vanity and folly repeated, with scarce a variation, in countless human lives."

"Well," said the American, "the fact of that repetition seems rather as if it were a law of human lives, don't it? We find ourselves in this world, and we must do as others do, and live as others live. Of course, I've read of people giving up all sorts of pleasures and comforts in this life for sake of another, but to me it seems only a mild form of madness. For instance, there's this new sect that's sprung up, who are going to revolutionize all creation—well, I've read heaps of their books, I've spoken even to some of their members, but I confess Theosophy seems as much of a jumble as any other creed. Look at their priests, their *yogis*, and *chelas*, and such-like humbugs! They say their Buddha is as divine as our Christ. Maybe he is—to them! But what strikes me is the absurdity of trying to get into another life while one has to live this. Fasting and sitting under a tree, and starving out all fleshly desires and impulses until the human body, instead of being handsome and muscular as Nature intended it to be, becomes a withered skeleton, subsisting on a few beans and a cup of water. Why, anybody could see visions and dream dreams that lived a life like that even for a year! But I want to know what's the good of it? I suppose if we get out of our natural life before our time, our place can't be ready for us in our next Karma, or whatever they call it. So we would martyrize ourselves to no purpose. These sort of people seem to me to be trying to steal a march over others, wanting to get a stage further on the road before the natural term of earth-life is over. A nice world this would be if we were all at that game."

" You have certainly read to some purpose," said the stranger ironically. " It is interesting to hear the deepest philosophy that has ever occupied the human mind summed up and dismissed as ridiculous. Let me, however, first point out a few mistakes in your judgment of this new 'sect' as you call it. In the first place it is not a sect in the common acceptation of the word, but rather a universal philosophy embracing all creeds, ranks, and denominations of men. It lays not the slightest stress on any of its followers martyrizing their bodies as you so glibly describe. You might just as well say that the Christian religion is only carried out by monks and nuns, because certain enthusiasts prefer to cut themselves adrift from the vanities of life. In all ages and in all religions there have been such enthusiasts. Even the prophets in your own Bible were men of this description, living in caves, subsisting only on the fruits and seeds of the earth, and giving themselves up to visions and dreams. What else have your canonized Saints done? Yet they are worshipped by a vast community of *apparently* sensible beings, as holy. It only shows that there are certain minds capable of penetrating the uselessness of a purely worldly existence, and finding it too hard to live a double life, that is to say, spiritual and material (a life only possible to the modern clergy), they seek refuge in seclusion and leave that outer life to those whom it satisfies and suits. As to the selfishness of such isolation, that is a matter no alien mind can quite determine, for the greatest Example of the religious life was strangely indifferent to human ties, nor ever displayed the weakness of human affection for earthly relatives, thus seeming to show that it is no sin to sacrifice earthly ties for a higher and holier existence. The disciples of the great Brotherhood are voluntary enthusiasts, free from the claims of human relationship, and offering themselves simply *as* disciples. They wrong no one by their choice. As for your last remark about endeavouring to steal a march on our fellow-men by seeking a higher place in the next state of existence, before we have done with this, I can only ask you to study something of the laws and doctrines of theosophical philosophy before deciding such an event is possible."

"Do you know much about them?" asked Mrs. Jefferson curiously.

"I know that they teach man the truest sense of his own responsibility. They prove to him an inexorable law by which he may lift himself from the level of the brute to the majesty of the God he now blindly worships."

"But so does Christianity," exclaimed Mrs. Jefferson astounded.

For the first time the stranger laughed.

"And is not true Christianity the highest and purest philosophy?" she said. "Only it is preached—not practised. Can you tell me that a single Christian land in this nineteenth century era is one whit purer or better in its spiritual or moral character than was Jerusalem a thousand years ago? Does it influence commerce, trade, governments, laws— even civilization? If it did, not one rule or law that binds the rotten fabric of civilized life together would stand for a single moment

Why? Because no one would lie; no one would cheat; no one would murder, either wholesale because of country prejudices, or retail because of private animosities. Everyone would be honest, charitable, merciful, and unselfish. You cling to a Faith that is almost barren of good works. You propagate it among ignorant savages whom you first rob of their lands, and then convert with guns and brandy bottles. How much of the reception of Christianity is due to the *latter* I will leave to the revelations of the first honest missionary whose report is not indebted to his income from the Society, a prospective pension, and his own personal weakness for the laudation of his fellow men. Show me a human being who can be honest to a conviction in the face of scorn and mockery, who never sought his *own* interest in the profession he embraced, but only the good of others for whom that profession was ostensibly established; who would speak truth in the Courts of Law, the House of Legislature, and the *salons* of Society; who would write—not for empty praise but from conviction—and follow art simply and purely to ennoble the mind, not pander to the lust of the eye and the greed of gold. Show me such men and such a nation, and I will acknowledge *there* Christianity has found its seat and fulfilled the purpose of its founder!"

"Oh," said the American, shrugging her shoulders with contempt, "of course, you are talking arrant nonsense! The thing's impossible. The world can't be turned into a monastery, and as long as people live they will always be overreaching each other, and deceiving each other. It's not possible to be perfectly honest, or perfectly truthful."

"Then," said the stranger quietly, as she sank back on her cushions, "do not blame even the poor *Yogi* under his tree if he has turned away sick and disgusted with the shams and vileness, and hypocrisies and evil, of the so-called civilized world. Remember that the country that holds him and thousands as foolish and superstitious, is the country that your boasted civilization has wrested from his race, and that *your* example as a Christian nation is ever before his eyes. Let his conduct determine it's influence!"

"Well," said Mrs. Jefferson, "talk of sermons in stones! Here's one in baths! I should like to know who you are. Seems to me you know everything, and have read everything, and seen most everything on the face of the earth. So few women begin to think of anything serious till they've forgotten their looks, that you must excuse my calling you an anomaly. Now do tell me you'll change your mind and join us to-night in the drawing - room. It's quite as selfish as *Yogaism* to keep talents like yours in the background."

The beautiful face grew cold and proud.

"You must pardon me," she said, "if I venture to consider myself the best judge of what you are pleased to call—talents. They are not of an order to benefit a hotel drawing-room."

"Oh!" said Mrs. Jefferson, feeling somewhat snubbed. "I'm sure people would be delighted to hear you talk, even if you did rub some of their pet foibles the wrong way. I've quite enjoyed this morning, I assure you. You've diverted my thoughts from my own ailments, and stimulated my digestion. I feel like eating lunch for once. And that reminds me I must begin to dress. My fringe takes a quarter of an hour to arrange."

She rose from the couch, her Turkish towelling drapery flowing far behind her small figure. Then she disappeared into her dressing-room.

When she emerged from thence, her fringe artistically curled, her face becomingly tinged with pearl-powder, her dress and appointments all combining to give her small person importance, and show a due regard to the exigencies of fashion, she found the couch which the mysterious stranger had occupied was vacant. She loitered about in the hope of seeing her emerge from one of the dressing-boxes, but she was disappointed, and as the luncheon gong was sounding through the hotel she reluctantly took her way through the carpeted corridors and turned into the main entrance, her mind in a curious condition of perplexity and excitement.

CHAPTER IV.

CONJECTURES.

MRS. Ray Jefferson, irrespective of a toilet of ruby velvet cut *en cœur*, and a display of diamonds calculated to make men thoughtful on the subject of speculation, and women envious on the subject of husbandly generosity (even when connected with Chemicals), was quite the feature of the Hotel drawing-room that night. She was full of her adventure of the morning, and her description of the beautiful stranger lost nothing from the picturesque language in which she clothed her narrative.

"It's very odd the Manager won't tell us her name," she rattled on. "I've done my level best to find out, but it's no good. I suppose she pays too well for him to risk betraying her. I'm sure she's a Russian Princess; she has a suite with her, and carries musicians and sculptors, and heaven knows who else, in her train."

It may be noticed that Mrs. Ray Jefferson had only heard of *a* sculptor and *a* musician, but she drifted into plurality by force of that irresistible tendency to exaggerate trifles which seems inherent in women who are given to scandal even in its mildest form.

People from all parts of the room gathered round her. A few seemed inclined to doubt her description of the stranger's personal charms, but when she applied to Mrs Masterman for confirmation, that lady, who was known to have a strict regard for truth in its most uncompromising form, emphatically agreed with her.

"Beautiful! I should think she was beautiful," she said, in her usual surly fashion. "But,"—and then came a series of those curious and condemnatory phrases with which a woman invariably finishes her praise of another woman's beauty, and which are too well known to be repeated.

"I did my best to try and persuade her to join us," continued Mrs. Jefferson, after duly agreeing with Mrs. Masterman that perhaps the stranger's hair was a shade too black, and her height too tall, and her complexion too pale —and that there *was* something uncanny in the expression of the dark wild eyes, "more like the eyes of a horse than a human being," was Mrs. Masterman's verdict. "But nothing would induce her. She says Society is all a sham. That we don't really amuse ourselves or enjoy ourselves, however much we pretend to! My word! doesn't she give it hot to everything. Policy, religion, diplomacy, worldliness, theology, art. It seems to me she knows everything, and has studied human life more accurately than the wisest philosopher I've ever heard of."

"And did you discuss all those subjects during the course of a Turkish Bath?" said a voice near her.

Mrs. Jefferson started. The gentleman who had spoken was a recent arrival. She only knew him as Colonel Estcourt. He was a singularly interesting-looking man, home from India on sick leave, and the maidens, and wives, and widows, of this polyglot assemblage at the Hotel were all inclined to admiration of his physical perfections, and to dissatisfaction at a certain coldness and disdainfulness of themselves, which, to use their mildest form of reproach, was " odd and unmilitary."

Mrs. Jefferson started slightly. "Oh, it's you, Colonel," she said. "Yes, we did talk about all those subjects, and I surmise if all of you people here heard her carry on against the way you live your lives, you'd feel rather small."

"Did you?" asked Mrs. Masterman unkindly.

The bath had not improved *her* complexion, and her left foot was paining her excessively. These two facts had not combined to sweeten the natural acerbity of her temper. Mrs. Ray Jefferson did not heed the question, or the smile it provoked on one or two feminine lips.

"I should like to know who she is," she persisted. "She's been in India too. I suppose you never met her, Colonel Estcourt? No one could forget her who had!"

That cold impassive face changed ever so slightly. "India," he said, "is a somewhat vague term, and covers a somewhat large area for a possible meeting-place. Your description, Mrs. Jefferson, is tantalizing in the extreme to a male mind, but I fail to recognise its charming original as any personal acquaintance."

"I suppose so," said the little American, discontentedly. "I'm just dying to know who she is, and therefore no one can tell me. Seems I shall have to call her 'the Mystery,' until she condescends to throw off this *incognita* business."

"But we are sure to see her," interposed Orval Molyneux, the young poet. "She must go out sometimes, I suppose."

"If you'll take my advice," said Mrs. Jefferson brusquely, "you won't try to see her, for it's my belief that she's not the woman any man can look at and forget, and you poets are mostly impressionable."

"Such a warning is only adding zest to temptation," said Colonel Estcourt, with a grave smile. "You really have aroused my curiosity in no small degree. But perhaps the mysterious beauty may not be so obdurate as you imagined. Why should she not show herself among us? It is contrary to all known rules of Nature for a beautiful woman to hide herself from the admiration her charms would exact. When those charms are coupled with mental gifts of so diverse and unusual a nature as Mrs. Jefferson has described, the probability is that seclusion is only a whim, unless indeed——"

He broke off abruptly. A certain look of disturbance and perplexity came into his deep grey eyes.

"Unless what?" queried Mrs. Jefferson, sharply. "You look as if you saw a vision. Unless she's committed a crime, were you going to say? She talked of some tragedy—

something that had upset her life, and affected her mental equilibrium."

"She said—that?" His face grew suddenly very pale. The firm mouth quivered beneath the fair thick moustache that shaded it.

"Yes," said Mrs. Jefferson, "Do tell, Colonel. What is it you suspect? A mystery—a secret crime? My, that would be interesting."

"Suspect!" he said, almost fiercely. "How should I suspect? What do you mean? I was only wondering if indeed she possessed one of those rare minds sufficient for their own happiness, and living an inner life of which the world knows nothing, and which, even if it knew, it could not comprehend."

"Ah," said Mrs. Jefferson, quickly. "Now this gets interesting. That's just the sort of way she talked, and I confess I got a bit out of my depth. But you, Colonel, you've come from the very land of it all. Do sit down and explain. Is the world going to be turned upside down? Are we to have a new religion, or rather an old one brought to light, that will upset what we've been hugging as truth for the last eighteen hundred years. We've been pretty crazy over spiritualism on our side of the water, but I guess this new philosophy can just make our mediums and *séance*-givers take a back seat. Isn't that so?"

"My dear madam," answered Colonel Estcourt, gravely, "you really must not call upon me to expound the doctrines of the East to the scoffers of the West. I know a little—a very little—of this school of philosophy; but I am not vain enough to attempt an explanation of its profound wisdom. The mysteries of Nature demand the deepest and most earnest consideration of the human mind. Do you think I could presume to rattle off a few explanations or give the key to certain problems just to satisfy the vague curiosity of an idle hour. I will only say one thing—it is a thing that cannot be too often repeated and thoroughly kept in memory. Every life has to live out itself, and work out for *itself* the higher mysteries that are shut within its own consciousness. No one can do that for it, any more than they could take its love, or its sorrows, or its misfortunes away, and bear them in its place. If humanity took that truth to heart, and lived according to the higher instead of the lower instincts, the world would be a very different place."

"But," objected a pretty feminine voice in the back-ground, "what about the obligations of position and society? I suppose the 'higher instinct' would tell us that amusements are a waste of time—vanity and vexation in fact—yet even they have a good result, they give employment, and help other folk to live. And it's a pleasant relief to be gay and frivolous. It's awfully fatiguing to be grave and good. Just look at us on Sundays. We're all more or less cross and disagreeable, and I'm sure no clergyman could honestly say that he wasn't heartily sick of droning and intoning that same eternal form embodied in the Church Service."

"The higher life," said Colonel Estcourt, gravely, "is not a matter of form. Far from it. It is an unceasing and inexhaustible pursuit; it has infinite gradations, and is full of infinite possibilities   Its tendency is to elevate all that is best, and eliminate all that is worst, in man."

"Oh!" cried Mrs. Jefferson with rapture, "I'm sure you ought to meet my 'Mystery.' That's just her sort of talk. I must say it sounds beautiful; but I shouldn't think it was practicable. It's a very hard thing to change people's ideas. When they've held them a certain time they get used to them, and don't like the trouble of altering."

"True," said Colonel Estcourt, "and therein lies the secret of all the misery and mistakes that have made the world what it is. The few enthusiasts and propagandists have always been confronted by that mountain of inertness, prejudice, and indolence, which the aggregate portion of all nations oppose to anything newer, or wiser, or better than the sloth and ignorance of the past."

"Well," laughed Mrs. Jefferson, "let's see what this new era will bring about. There's a grand opening for it, and it has this advantage—people are much more dissatisfied with old creeds, and much more eager for new, than they have ever been. The reins are slack, if only there's a firm and judicious hand to seize them."

"Suppose," drawled Mr. Ray Jefferson, who had the rare virtue of being an admirable listener to any controversy or discussion. "Suppose, my dear, we have a game of poker."

"Agreed," laughed his wife. "This meeting's adjourned, Colonel Estcourt. Will you join us."

He shook his head. "No," he said, "I'm going out on the terrace to smoke."

"And meditate on the Unknown?" queried the little American. "Perhaps you'll see her at her window. I wish you luck."

He did not answer, but his brow clouded and his face grew anxious and absorbed. In his heart those light words echoed with a thrill of mingled pain and dread. "If it should be," he said to himself." · "My God—if it should be she?"

CHAPTER V.

"LOVE."

THE stars were gleaming above the dusky pine trees. The soft December air, mild as spring on that sheltered coast, scarcely stirred the drooping boughs that over-shadowed the terrace. Colonel Estcourt lit his cigar, and began to pace with slow and thoughtful steps beneath the many lighted windows of the great building. Mrs. Jefferson's words haunted him, despite his efforts to dispel them. One of those windows belonged to the room where this strange and beautiful woman might even now be seated. Why did he picture to himself the pale exquisite face—the full dark eyes—the lovely rippling hair—as if they were charms already recognized and remembered. Why?—save that when he had heard their description they had struck home to his memory with a shock of pain, and a feverish dread that longed yet feared to find itself realized. To and fro—to and fro—he paced the terraced walk, and again and again his eyes sought that long line of light above his head.

There was a strange stillness in the brooding air—that mysterious hush, which is the music of night's gentle footsteps, and insensibly its soothing influence stole over the unquiet of his restless thoughts—the warring powers of soul and sense grew silent and at rest.

Then something—a sound sweet as song —yet without the vibratory passion of a human voice—seemed to float out of the darkness and hold his ear enchained like a spell. It was the divinest beauty of music, divinely interpreted, and it seemed to him as he listened that all the discord and woe and misery that oppressed his earthly senses, disappeared and died away into the very perfection of peace.

He stood there quite silent—quite motionless—waiting, so it seemed to himself, for some fuller revelation to which these exquisite sounds were but a prelude.

It was a matter of no surprise when he quietly lifted his dreamy glance to the stone balcony above, and saw there, in the soft glow of light from the rooms beyond, the fair form of the woman he had expected to see.

A faint tremor of fear and apprehension thrilled his heart, but it died away as a low remembered voice stole through the space that parted him from a visible form he had never thought to see again.

"I told you we should meet. But I scarcely thought it would be so soon. Will you come up here, or shall I join you?"

The voice and greeting roused him. He bared his head and bent low to the speaker in a deeper homage than that of conventional courtesy.

"Is it really you, Princess? And may I be permitted to join you?"

The mute sign of assent showed him also a flight of steps leading up from the terrace to the balcony. A moment, and he was by her side.

No ordinary greeting passed between them. Perhaps none could have conveyed what that long silent gaze did; seeming to go straight to the heart of each, full of memories that time had softened, but sad with the sadness that is in all deep human love.

"A strange meeting-place," she said. "Yet why more strange than the mountains of the East, or the lonely plains of the Desert, the steppes of Russia, or the house-tops of Damascus?"

"You read my thoughts, as ever," he said. "I must confess that it seemed strange to see you here, treading the narrow path of English conventionalism, after—after—— "

"I know," she said. "But life is full of the unexpected. You do not ask how these five years have been spent. The years that have changed the dreamy enthusiastic girl into a woman such as you see before you."

"I do not ask," he said, his voice vibrating beneath an emotion he could not conceal, "because it can be no pleasure to me to learn. Do you forget what I told you? Do you think that the memory of these five years is a pleasant one for me? Against my prayers, against my warnings, you chose your own life. Are you free—now?"

"No," she said, in a strange stifled voice, "never *that*—never while I wear the shackles of humanity!" She sank suddenly down in a low seat, and buried her face in her hands. "Oh," she cried, faintly, "if I could tell you —if I only dared; but I cannot! My bondage is deeper—my chains are heavier. Sometimes I think those years were only a dream— a horrible, frightful dream—but then, again, I *know* they were not."

"What do you mean?" he asked, his voice sharp with terror, for this shame and remorse that convulsed her, and made her one with the common weakness of her common womanhood, was something altogether different to the supremacy she had always shown in her proud girlhood.

"I cannot tell you," she said, "I dare not."

"Do you forget," he said, severely, "that if I *wish* to know, I shall learn it?"

"Not now," she said, suddenly, and raised her face and looked calmly, yet not defiantly, back at him with her great, sad, and most lovely eyes. "I have passed beyond your power," she went on. "Beyond most human influence, I might say"—then she shuddered and her eyes sank again. "But oh!" she cried, "at what a cost!—at what a cost!"

He felt as if his heart grew suddenly chill and stony. "I believe you are right," he said; "my power is gone—yours is the strongest now."

He was silent for a few moments. "One question only," he then said; "I don't wish to pry into your past. It is enough that we have met—for that would never have taken place if you had not needed me. So much I know. Your marriage—was it as I foretold?"

"It was worse," she said, bitterly—"a million times worse! Body and soul, how I have suffered! And yet, as I told you then, *it had to be.*"

"I did not believe it then," he said stormily; "I refuse to believe it now. Your misery was self-created. You voluntarily degraded yourself. What result could there be? Only suffering and shame."

"The good of others," she answered mournfully. "You cannot see it yet; but I know —it was foretold me. I did my work there. Sometimes I hope it is finished; but I do not know. One can never tell; at any time the summons may come again. God help me if it does."

"Is your life in danger, then?" he asked, and again that chill and horror seemed to thrill the pulses of his beating heart.

"My life!" She lifted her eyes and looked back at his with something intensely mournful in her gaze. "As if *that* mattered! What is my life to me now, any more than it was then? Did I count the cost—did I call it a sacrifice? Life—the mere material actual life of the body—has never weighed with me for one moment. And yet," she added, in a dull, strange voice, "I failed at the crucial test! Failed!—I, who had denied to myself all woman's weakness, all mortal love, all fleshly vanities—failed! I am no more now than the veriest beginner on the path. I, who deemed myself so wise!"

Then she rose and came close to him, and laid her white hand on his arm. "That," she said, "is why I needed you again. You can help me—you can tell me where and how I failed."

That light touch thrilled his veins like sorcery. He bent his head and passionately kissed the white, soft hand. "You failed, oh, my Princess! because you are still mortal woman. Thank Heaven for it! You failed because memory and love were still strong in your heart. You failed—and I am by your side once more. Oh, let the past be forgotten! Brief is life, but love is its Paradise, and into that Paradise our feet once strayed. Fate stayed them on the threshold. But now—now——"

She raised her white face. "Do not deceive yourself," she said. "You have always loved me too well—but I——"

"Only *let* me love you!" he whispered passionately. "It is honour enough. All the wide earth holds no other woman such as you. Having once known you, there has never been a disloyal thought within my heart. Read it—see for yourself."

"I read it," she said, "even while the music was sounding in your ears, as you stood on the terrace there below; even while you moved amidst that chattering, flippant throng, and heard what they said of me. No, dear friend. You have nothing in that great frank, loyal soul to hide. But I—there is something that whispers I shall only bring you suffering. 1 am not for mortal love. True, I cannot see beyond, but Fear meets me on the threshold. The hour I gave myself to you would bring you an evil I dimly realise. I cannot foretell, and I cannot avert it; but it is there. It lurks like a hidden foe where our lives should join . . . . No, no!—do not tempt me. Happiness is not for me, as we count it on the earth plane."

"And in the next I may lose you altogether. Oh listen—listen, and let the woman defy the priestess. Give me your love, and, even with Death as its bridal gift I shall receive it as the deepest joy of earth."

"There," she said sadly, "speaks the mortal. Passion sways your senses. You too will lose your powers—and for what?—a few brief years of joy—a longer darkness—then the old weary round—the old sad effort to climb the long stairway from the bottom rung that once you proudly spurned. It was not this that Channa taught us in the sweet peace of our youth—it was not this for which our souls thirsted, and to which our faces were set."

"Channa is dead, and to the dead all is peace. Even he said that Life's one good gift was Love."

"True, but not selfish love. 'The feet of the soul must be washed in the blood of the heart.' Love to all humanity—to the poor— the sad—the suffering. Love, even to the Fate that gives us sorrow and misfortune. Love to the eternal and immutable. Love for all that is purest and best in each life with which we mingle. Such a love is not sensual —not earthly. It gives without necessity of return; it is the soul's devotion, not the

heart's impulse.   But you are not content
with loving me, you claim mine in return,
and so far as I have lost or you have gained
a firmer foothold since last we met, so far you
can compel my lower nature to answer yours.
We have loved before, and unhappy was our
fate.   Once more we meet, and your cry is
still for me.   And I——"

She ceased ; her arms fell to her side.   Her
face, lovely beyond all mere mortal loveliness,
looked back to his yearning, passionate gaze.
Had she been temptress, devil, saint, there
could have been but one answer from the
throbbing heart and leaping pulse of manhood.   He caught her to his heart, and his
lips drank from hers the sweetness that only
earthly passion drains from earthly love.

She did not resist.   She lay there like a
white lily in the moonlight, but her lips were
cold as marble and her eyes held the mute
sorrow of despair, not the rapture of a
granted joy.

*   *   *   *   *

CHAPTER VI.

ENCHANTMENT.

WHEN a proud woman yields to the entreaties
of a lover, she yields with a grander humility,
a more complete self-surrender, than one to
whom coquetry and conquests are natural
attributes of vanity.

The Princess Zairoff, to whom men's admiration was as familiar as the air of Heaven,
who possessed rank and wealth and loveli-

ness such as dower few women, had yet never granted to one human being a sign of tenderness, or unveiled, so to speak, the deep strange depths of her strange nature, to any beseechment.

But now, for one brief hour she threw back the portals of emotion. She was a woman, pure and simple. The man beside her was the one man in the world to whom her memory had been faithful. Boy and girl they had known each other in years long past. As boy and girl they had shared in the same tastes, and been penetrated with the same desires for the Mystic and the Unknown.

Living in a remote part of India under very careless guardianship, and with no one to care for their pursuits, or remark them, they had made the acquaintance of a learned and somewhat mysterious native, and from his lips they first heard some hints of the wonders that nature reveals to the earnest student. As time went on they were separated—the boy was sent to England, the girl remained in the East. When they met again he was a young lieutenant in an infantry regiment stationed at one of the most popular stations of a popular Presidency, and she was the reigning queen of the same station. Again fate parted them. Two years went by. Their next meeting was in Egypt, where she was travelling with her guardian.

Julian Estcourt had learnt his heart's secret by then, but there was a coldness, a strangeness, about the girl who had been his boyhood's friend that kept him back from anything bearing the imputation of love-making.

Much as they were together, long and fre-
quent as were their talks, those talks were yet
curiously impersonal for their age and sex,
and, however much the young man's heart
might throb with its hidden passion, there yet
lay between them a barrier, a restraint, light,
yet strangely strong, and his lips never dared
betray the secret of his long-cherished devotion.

Another separation — another meeting.
Time had worked changes in both. She was
a beautiful woman, proud, cold, queenly—
he had acquired strength of character, loftier
ideals, and a sense of the value of intellectual
gifts, which had kept him singularly free from,
and indifferent to, the temptations of the
senses. He had learnt to drink mental
stimulants with avidity. Had made one or
two brilliant successes in literature, and was
looked upon as a supremely " odd fish," by
his brother officers.

That third meeting decided his fate. He
spoke out his love, spurred on by a rivalry he
had good cause to dread, but spoke to no
purpose. Calmly, though with a sorrow she
did not attempt to disguise, she told her old
playmate and friend that her choice was
made. She was going to marry the old,
vicious, and fabulously wealthy Russian
Prince, Fédor Ivanovitch Zairoff. She made
no pretence of caring for the man who out of
a host of suitors she had selected to wed.
When her young lover stormed and upbraided
her she only raised those wonderful stag-
like eyes to his face and said:

" I have a reason, Julian. I cannot explain

it. I dare not say more. Believe me I could not make you happy, *it would not be permitted.*"

And having long ago learnt that arguments were utterly useless before *that* formula, he had to stand aside—to crush back a strong and unconquerable passion—to see her pass from his sight and knowledge—and to bear his life as best he could, with that feeling in his heart of having staked all on one throw, and lost, that makes so many men desperate and vicious. That it did not make Julian Estcourt so was entirely due to great strength of moral character, and a belief in the responsibilities with which life is charged, and for the abuse of which it is destined to suffer in future states or conditions, as well as in its present.

If such belief were universally accepted and pursued, we should soon cease to hear those ridiculous and humiliating phrases with which popular favourites are extenuated for the reckless and disgraceful waste of mind, energy, and usefulness, occasioned by some trifling disappointment or misfortune. There would be no more sins glossed over as " sowing wild oats," and " having his fling," or " driven to the bad," because once an individual feels he is responsible to *himself* for undue physical indulgences — for laws of natural life set at naught, and spiritual impulses disregarded—he will try to emerge from the slough of evil, and he will learn with startling rapidity to value all joys of the senses less and less. There can be no high order of morality without this sense of responsibility, for when a man feels he is mould-

ing his own character, forming as it were
fresh links in the chain of endurance, adding
by every act and thought and word to that
personality he is bound to confront as *himself*,
to re-inhabit as himself, and to judge as
himself, then life rises into an importance
that words cannot convey, but which the soul
alone recognises and feels in those better
moments that are mercifully granted to each
and all of us.

So Julia Estcourt took up his burden—
saddened, aged, embittered perhaps, but not
one whit more inclined to squander the gifts
of life or the fruits of discipline than he had
been in his dreamy, studious youth.

He neither sought distraction in evil and
dissipated courses, nor death by any of those
foolhardy and rash exploits which have far
too often been glorified as " courage " or
" pluck."

He was graver, more reticent, more studious
than of yore, and he found his reward, though
few even of his intimate associates were aware
of his abnormal gifts, or his superior knowledge.   Such was the man who, still in the
prime of life's best years, still with thirst
unslaked for that one divine draught of love
which, once at least, is offered to mortal lips,
stood now in the soft December moonlight by
the side of the woman he had worshipped for
long in secret and in pain, and cried aloud in
triumph to his heart, " At last happiness is
mine ! "

His whole consciousness was pervaded with
a sense of ecstacy that seemed to make all
past pain and regret sink into utter insigni-

ficance. To stand there by her side, to drink in that wonderful beauty of face and form, was a joy that brought absolute forgetfulness of everything outside and apart from its new and magical acquisition. The world was forgotten. Even the possibility of a formal and imperative ceremonial by which his newly-won treasure must be secured to himself at last, barely flashed across his consciousness. He did not trouble himself to put it into words. He listened to the brief disjointed fragments of her speech—fragments which gave a dim picture of her life in these empty years of division. Now and then he spoke of himself. She listened. Once she turned to him with an impulse of tenderness strange in one so cold and self-possessed.

" Ah ! " she cried, softly, " I have made you suffer . . . . but it was not my will . . . . Oh, always believe that . . . And I will give you compensation. . . . I can promise it —now."

They seemed to him the sweetest words that ever fell from mortal lips, and no less sweet —though infinitely puzzling—was that exquisite humility with which she crowned the wonder of her self-surrender. Yet even as he heard his brain grew bewildered—his senses seemed to reel. Strange thoughts and shapes seemed to hover around him, and all the soft, dim space of night appeared a black and peopled horror. For a moment he felt that consciousness was forsaking him . . . . that the shock of this unexpected joy was beyond his strength to bear. Dizzy and sick he swayed suddenly forwards. . . . A cool hand touched his brow—a voice reached his ear. With a mighty effort he shook off the paralysing weakness, and sank down by the side of his enchantress.

"Is it a dream?" he murmured, vaguely; "shall I wake to-morrow and know you have mocked me again?"

"Nay, my beloved," she whispered; "this —is no dream. . . . Never again shall I mock you. I am but a woman now who loves. Earth holds no weaker thing.

*   *   *   *   *

When Julian Estcourt entered the public drawing-room, nearly two hours after he had left it, several curious eyes turned towards him. The card-players had finished their game and broken up into various groups. A few men were yawning and apparently meditating a retreat to the smoking-room. No one seemed particularly energetic, but the entrance of that tall soldierly figure struck a new note of interest in the languid assemblage. He seemed to bring—as it were—a breeze of vitality, a sense of freshness and energy along with him from the starlit air and the pine-scented woods. His head was erect, his eyes shone with the radiance of happiness, a certain sense of pride—of triumph—and yet of deep intense content, was in his aspect and his smile.

Mrs. Ray Jefferson, her spirits still un-impaired by losses at "poker," was the first to remark audibly on the change.

"Why, Colonel!" she said. "Have *you* been having a Turkish Bath? Guess you look as fresh and perky as if you'd taken a new lease of life."

He laughed. " The only bath I have taken," he said, " is one of moonlight. You should all be out on the terrace. Far healthier and more enjoyable than these hot, gas-lit rooms, I assure you."

" The terrace," said Mrs. Jefferson, looking at him with a sudden stern accusing glance. " Ladies and gentlemen, what did I tell you? I—do—believe——"

She paused dramatically, every eye turned fully and searchingly upon the handsome face and erect figure so calmly and easily confronting this sudden criticism.

" Well?" he said at last. " What is it you believe?"

" You've seen—her," burst out Mrs. Jefferson eagerly. " Now Colonel, no tricks—plain yes or no; I'm certain sure you've seen her—my Mystery. Haven't you?"

" I will not pretend," he said, " to misunderstand you. I have met an old friend, and I hope soon to have the pleasure of introducing her to you all. Not with any mystery about her, as our American friend seems determined to suppose, but simply as the Princess Zairoff—of whom you may have heard before this."

There was a buzz—a stir—a confused murmur. " Heard of her—I should think so. You never mean to say she's _here_? I thought she was in Russia——"

" Gracious!" almost shrieked Mrs. Jefferson. " Why it was her husand who died so mysteriously, on the eve of that awful conspiracy. You never mean to say, Colonel Estcourt, that you know her. Why she's one of the celebrities of Europe, and to come here, to this quiet place—and *incognito?*"

"Do you not think," he said, "that the fact of being quiet and unknown would just be the one fact she would appreciate? I hope I am not claiming too much from your courtesy when I say that the privilege of her society can only be obtained by a due regard to her wishes in that respect. She wishes only to be known as Madame Zairoff, here"

"I'm sure," exclaimed Mrs. Jefferson eagerly, "I'm only too willing to promise anything for the privilege of seeing her Isn't that the general opinion also?"

There was a murmur of assent, specially eager on the part of the men.

"I can only assure you," continued Colonel Estcourt gravely, "that you will not regret the slight inconvenience of repressing personal curiosity, for Madame Zairoff is a woman whose gifts and graces are of a marvellous nature and calculated to delight the most critical society. As Mrs. Jefferson told us, she is here for her health. It is an incident we cannot deplore if we are to benefit by her society."

"You'd better all look out for your hearts, gentlemen," laughed Mrs. Jefferson gaily and excitedly. "I assure you I don't believe there's another woman in the world like her. I've seen her under trying circumstances, and I give you my word of honour that a woman who can preserve any charm of personal appearance under the ordeal of a Turkish Bath——"

There came a discreet little cough from the neighbourhood of Mrs. Masterman. The little American stopped abruptly.

"I'd best say no more," she said. Then she laughed. "All the same, if you only could see us——"

CHAPTER VII.

CURIOSITY.

THERE was suppressed but general excitement throughout the hotel all the next day.

Someone had caught sight of the Princess Zairoff, who had driven out after luncheon in a low open carriage with three horses harnessed abreast in Russian fashion, that went like the wind. Colonel Estcourt was beside her, and curiosity was rife as to how he should have known her, and whether accident only was responsible for the meeting of two people, one of whom had come from Russia, and the other from India, to this prosaic English nook. *for their health.*

Mrs. Masterman sniffed ominously, as one who scents scandal and impropriety in facts that do not adapt themselves to every-day rules of life. A few other women, suffering from one or other of the fashionable complaints in vogue at this season, agreed with her, that "it certainly looked very odd."

They did not specify the "it," but they were quite convinced of the oddity. It did not occur to them to reflect that there was not the slightest reason for any mystery on the part of the Princess, she being perfectly free and untrammelled, or that Colonel Estcourt had been singularly gloomy and depressed before Mrs. Jefferson's graphic description of the mysterious beauty attracted his notice.

There is a certain class of people who always shake their heads, and purse up their lips, at the mere suggestion of "chance," or "accident," having a fortunate or happy application. They do not apply the same train of reasoning to the reverse side of the picture; the bias of their nature is evidently suspicious. These are the minds that refuse to credit those little misfortunes of picnic and pleasure parties, by which young people lose themselves in mysterious ways, and get into wrong boats and carriages, and generally contrive to upset the plans of their elders, when these plans have been framed with a deeper regard for rationality than for romance. Mrs. Masterman belonged to this class, which doubtless has its uses, though those uses are not plainly evident on the surface of life; she spent the day in gloomy hints, and mysterious shakes of the head, and insinuations that no good was ever known to spring from a superabundance of feminine charms, which, in the course of nature, must have an evil tendency. and be productive of overweening vanity, extravagance, and even immorality.

Still, even evil prognostications cannot quell the fires of curiosity in the female breast, and every woman in the hotel made her toilette with special care on this eventful evening, as befitting one who owed it to her sex to vindicate even the smallest personal attraction in the presence of rivalry. Colonel Estcourt was not at dinner, so his presence did not restrain comment and speculation, and the tongues did quite as much work as the knives and forks.

"I do wonder what sort of gown she'll wear," sighed Mrs. Ray Jefferson, who was attired in a "creation" of the great French man-milliner, accursed by husbands of fashionable wives, and whose power is only another note in that ascending scale of absurdity struck by the hands of fashion.

"Perhaps she won't come down in the drawing-room at all," said Mrs. Masterman spitefully, after listening for some time to the remarks around her. "Colonel Estcourt did not specify any particular night."

"Oh, I'm sure she'll come," said Mrs. Jefferson, whose nature was specially happy in always assuring her of what she desired. "I've got an impression that she will—they never fail me. You know I've a singularly magnetic organization. A great spiritualist in Boston once told me I only needed developing to exhibit extraordinary powers. But I hadn't the time or the patience to go in thorougly for psychic development. Besides it's really a very exacting pursuit."

"Exacting rubbish!" exclaimed Mrs Masterman impatiently, "I can't stand all that bosh about higher powers, and developing magnetism. Of course there are a set of people who'd believe anything that seemed to give them a superior organization ; it's only another way of pandering to human vanity. Spiritualism is perfect rubbish. I've seen and heard enough of it to know. I once held a séance at my house, just to convince myself as to its being a trick or not. I was told that the medium could materialize spirit forms. I, of course, asked some people to meet him, and we selected a room and put him behind a screen as he desired, and there we all sat in the dark, like so many fools, for about half-an-hour.——"

"Well," interposed Mrs. Jefferson eagerly, "and did you have any manifestation ?"

"Oh, yes," laughed the gouty sufferer grimly, "a very material one indeed. By some accident the medium knocked down the screen just after we'd seen a spirit face floating *above* it. In the confusion some one struck a light, and there was our medium —standing on the chair without his coat, and wrapping some transparent India muslin about himself, which had been dipped in phosphorus I believe, so that it gave out a curious shimmering light in the dark. You may suppose *I* never went in for materialistic séances again."

"Still," said Mrs. Jefferson, "although you may have been tricked, it doesn't stand to reason that spiritualism *is* trickery. I've come from the very core and centre of it—so to speak. I've been at more séances than I could count, and I've seen tests applied that *prove* the manifestations are genuine. Still there are heaps of professional mediums who are not to be depended on, I grant. If you want to know the truth of spiritualism, you can always work it out for yourself. That's quite possible, only it's a deal of trouble."

"I don't believe in it," reiterated Mrs. Masterman stubbornly. "All mediums are cheats and humbugs."

"Oh!" said Mrs. Jefferson. "If it comes to exceptions laying down the rule, where are we? The other day a clergyman was taken before the courts for drunkenness, but I suppose you're not going to say all clergymen are drunkards. A doctor poisoned a patient by mistake, but surely we're not to class our dear medical men as poisoners and murderers on that account. It's just the same with any abnormal or extraordinary facts that set up a new theory for investigation. Impostors are sure to creep in, and the lazy and the indifferent and the sceptical call their exposure 'results.' Depend on it we don't half investigate subjects now-a-days, and we suffer for it by giving place and opportunity for the development of a certain class of beings who prey on our credulity, and make profit out of our indolence and superstition."

"There's something in spiritualism, you bet," drawled the nasal voice of Mr. Ray Jefferson. "I've had messages written to me, and things said that no third person could possibly have known about."

"Ah, slate writing," sneered Mrs. Masterman. "I've seen that too. Just another trick."

"How do you explain that?" asked Mrs. Jefferson quickly.

"Well, this way. I went to two or three different mediums so as to test them all. I found they had no objections to bringing your own slates and writing your own questions, but while they held the slate under the table they kept you talking to distract your attention, and from time to time they got convulsive jerks and movements by which it was quite possible for them to see what was written. Then you heard a scratching (the medium probably had a little bit of pencil in his finger-nail), and your answer was given you. Well, let that pass for what it's worth, but I always noticed the medium asked if I wouldn't like a message, and when I said 'yes,' he brought out *his own slate*."

"But," said Mrs. Jefferson, "didn't he let you examine it first?"

"Oh yes, and wiped it over with a damp cloth. Then it was held under the table, and in a few seconds covered with 'spirit-writing.' But *I* found out afterwards that you can buy slates with a *false cover*, this cover fits within the frame and is exactly like the other side of the slate, but, *your spirit-message is already written*, a touch makes the cover drop off, the medium covers it with his foot in case you should look under the table, out comes the slate, and there you are!"

"Oh," said Mrs. Jefferson angrily, "it's plain you've only been to the charlatans and impostors of spiritualism. Why, I've had

a message written in a *locked* slate while I
held the key and held the slate too. What
do you say to that?"

" I've only your word for it," said Mrs.
Masterman sarcastically. " My slates were
never locked."

" And I've only *your* word for what you've
told us," answered Mrs. Jefferson with rising
wrath. " I suppose my evidence may be as
trustworthy."

" Well," interposed another voice, " my
view of spiritualism is, that it's an intensely
humiliating idea after you've done with this
world to be at the beck and call of any other
human being who can make you go through
a variety of tricks, as if you were a perform-
ing dog, in order to convince people still in
the body that there is another life. If that
other life permits us to come back here and
play tambourines, and knock furniture about,
and write silly and ambiguous messages on
slates, I don't—myself—think it's a very
desirable one."

This view of the question produced a blank
silence. It proceeded from a gentleman who
was supposed to be a little " odd "—partly
because he spoke seldom, and then with a
startling originality, on any subject of discussion.

Mr. and Mrs. Ray Jefferson looked at one
another, somewhat dismayed. Mrs. Masterman smiled triumphantly, the young poet
murmured something vague about the inestim-
able beauty of sublime " mysteries," but the
subject was temporarily extinguished. The
only side hitherto considered had been the

'phenomenal,' and people—once the idea was originated—felt really inclined to think that after all, when they quitted the earth plane, it would not be a very elevating prospect to find themselves dragged back to give *séances* and perform tricks like a French poodle in order to convince their friends and relatives that they were *still in existence !*

The conversation only went on in subdued murmurs, and presently there was a feminine move towards the drawing-room.

Once there the great subject as to whether Madame Zairoff would or would not appear that evening, was again freely discussed. That it was an equally interesting probability to the sterner sex was soon made evident by the unusual alacrity with which they joined the circle. They broke up into groups and knots, scattered through the length of the handsome, brilliantly lighted room, but a curious restlessness was apparent; no one settled down to cards or music. Even the " odd " individual moved about and dropped cynical remarks along the route of his progress, instead of sitting down to back-gammon as was his wont. A few other misguided individuals, of the male sex, offered and accepted bets *sotto voce* on the chances of the Unknown appearing.

At last, when expectation had been strained almost to breaking point, it was set at rest. The doors were thrown open, and, lightly leaning on Colonel Estcourt's arm, appeared Mrs. Jefferson's much talked of, and beautiful " Mystery."

CHAPTER VIII

SURPRISE.

An involuntary hush fell upon the whole assemblage. Not a man or woman there but felt their breath come a little quicker, their hearts beat with suppressed excitement, as that perfect figure, with its magical indolent grace, swept slowly through the room and into their midst.

It was the usual homage paid to Princess Zairoff, for she possessed that rare and delicate mixture of indifference, languor, and disdain that is in itself a distinction, and makes ordinary womanhood and beauty suddenly feel coarse and commonplace.

She paused before Mrs. Ray Jefferson, and greeted her with a soft indescribable grace, and after a few minutes' conversation permitted herself to be introduced to a few of the group around the little American. That perfect ease of manner, which held not a vestige of condescension, soon exerted its charm. One after another drew near that envied circle, anxious to pick up some stray pearl of speech from those lovely lips. The women forgot to be envious, because she never for one moment forgot or ignored them. Even gouty Mrs. Masterman found that her ailment had been remembered, and was sympathetically enquired about in a way to which she was entirely unaccustomed. The poet talked as if he drew in inspiration with every glance from those starry eyes, the musician at her request moved to the piano and played some of his "Music of the Future," and it no longer seemed incomprehensible. A sense of exhilaration, of pleasure, of content, spread through the group, and animated discussion, and gave even ordinary conversation a sudden grace and charm.

It was to be expected before the evening was over, that that conversation would ascend by natural gradations from the ordinary to the intellectual, yet no one could tell exactly how or when it began to do so, any more than they could describe the strange yet clear logic by which this one woman set to rights various perplexing problems, and gave the key as it were to a nobler and higher order of eclectic philosophy than they had yet ventured upon.

To Mrs. Ray Jefferson, that discussion in the Baths had acted as the stimulus of an olive to the palate. She was all eagerness to resume it.

"I hope, Madame Zairoff," she said, in her brisk, lively, fashion, "that you will give me a little enlightenment about what you said yesterday. This is just a leisure time with most of us, and I suppose mental culture is not incompatible with hygienic pursuits."

"Assuredly not," said the Princess, smiling "The more you cultivate the mind the less you feel or care for the ailments of the body, and to give those ailments even occasional insignificance, is to first forget, and then banish them. If you draw your mind away from the thought of pain, you cease to feel pain."

"But that would require a far stronger mental capacity than we possess," said Mrs. Masterman. Then she suddenly remembered that she had not felt a single gouty twinge the whole evening, because her mental consciousness had been unusually excited. This remembrance made her grow suddenly thoughtful and attentive to the discussion.

"I think," said Princess Zairoff, gently; "that we all make a great mistake in setting any absolute limit to our mental capacity. It is quite within our own power to dwarf or extend it. If we are content to rest satisfied with a small amount of knowledge we can do so, and even cease to suffer in our own self-esteem by feeling we are stupid, or indolent, or ignorant. Our perceptions are gradually blunted, and society is kind enough to case most of its remarks and opinions in a sugar-coating, so that the real truth never reaches us. We gradually find, then, that an opinion that soothes our personal vanity and self-esteem is a very pleasant opinion. So long as we cherish that falsehood, so long do we blunt our faculties of progress Now it seems a very extraordinary thing to me, who have long been accustomed to investigate and dissect the psychic side of nature, to find such numbers and numbers of people who don't believe in *any psychic laws at all*, far less care to investigate them as knowledge. The reason is simply this, that they all are convinced that *one* trivial, petty earth-life is the one life for, which they were created and are responsible, therefore the only one they feel bound to investigate."

She paused and looked at the circle of grave and wondering faces.

" You have heard of the law of Karma, I suppose ? " she said.

There was a murmur, vague, spontaneous, or doubtful, according to the amount of comprehension excited by the question.

" It is a pity," resumed the Princess, " that it is not more generally understood. What is the difficulty ? I learnt it in my childhood just as your English children learn their catechism. You have taken up the doctrine of Evolution very strongly, but Karma is its very leading law, so to speak. Man is perpetually working out and developing afresh the energies, aspirations, and character with which his spirit was originally endowed. He becomes, as it were, the product of the better part of himself, that struggles to the surface again and again during periods of incarceration in the flesh."

" Then you would convey that we all live over and over again ? "

" Most certainly. It is the only rational way to account for the injustice, the sorrows, and the miseries of earth. It gives long opportunities for the modification of character; it acts as retribution to the evil and the vicious and the selfish ; it gives a far deeper sense of responsibility than the shallow acceptance of mere creeds, because a man's good or evil deeds become a series of actions with inevitable consequences. If you teach him that he can throw off the results of a bad life, and of all it has entailed upon his fellowman, by a brief spell of penitence, or a blind, irrational faith in the sacrifice of a Being he has neglected and ignored during the greater part of that life, you really are only pandering to the selfish and cowardly side of his nature."

A little shudder ran through the group at these bold words. Mrs. Ray Jefferson lifted her head and cast glances of triumph about, as one who should say, "I told you she would shock you all!".

There was scarcely a man or woman there who did not attend church on Sundays, and who had not managed to make a comfortable compact between the tenets of religion and the demands of social and worldly pleasures. Not one who, if taken to task on the momentous subject of a spiritual future, could have given any rational explanation of why he or she held certain vague ideas on the subject of salvation, or put off the deeper consideration of the subject to some indefinite period when they would have had their fill of vanities, and lost either the means or the desire to pursue them.

And yet there was a subtle *frou-frou* of rustling skirts as the women drew slightly away, and a decided appearance of discomfort on the faces of the men, to whom an unpleasant truth was suddenly and sharply conveyed, and who found themselves strangely powerless to combat, or argue out its real meaning.

CHAPTER IX.

DISCUSSION.

COLONEL ESTCOURT came to the rescue.

"No doubt," he said, "the subject and this view of the subject seems a little strange to our friends here. We must remember they have not been accustomed to hear it freely discussed, as we have "

"It *is* strange," said Mrs. Jefferson, rallying her energies, "but we should not shirk its consideration for that reason. I quite agree with Madame Zairoff that people don't think half seriously enough of their real natures, the mysterious inner *something* which we all feel we possess, but whose voice we stifle in the din of the world. And yet," she added, sighing pathetically as she looked at the great Worth's ' creation,'—" the vanities are very pleasant. Why should we turn anchorites ?"

"There is not the slightest necessity to do that," said the princess, smiling at the unuttered thought she had read in that glance. "Far from it. The gravest duties of life are generally those that meet us in the world, and are called forth by our actions in that world. All lives are not meant to be isolated, and certainly none for the whole period of earth-life. A person would have to be very sure that he was *free* to cut himself adrift from his fellows before he would even be permitted to do it."

" Permitted!" echoed Mrs Jefferson, rather vaguely. " But by whom ? "

" The teachers of occult science," answered the Princess Zairoff.

" But who are they ? " exclaimed the little American.

" That I cannot tell you," she answered, gravely. " They exist, and their influence is already beginning to make itself felt. But it would be a poor triumph to unveil the highest wisdom that humanity can ever learn, in order to satisfy the idle and the curious, and the lovers of marvels Those who desire to learn can always do so, but nothing is forced upon you, or even obtruded. I should not have opened my lips on the subject had you not expressed a desire to hear something about it."

" I suppose," said Mrs. Jefferson, eagerly, " you yourself are a believer in occultism ? "

" Madame Zairoff is a great deal more than that," said Colonel Estcourt; " she is one of its most earnest students and most ardent votaries. If you knew half of her marvellous powers you would congratulate yourselves upon being permitted to receive her, unless, indeed," he added, with a questioning glance at the beautiful woman beside him, " she has a fancy to make converts."

The men became eager of entreaties to her so made, but the women held back a little.

Princess Zairoff, however, assured them she had no intention of proselytizing. " It is quite true I am deeply interested in this subject," she said, "but I should be sorry to bore you all with my views, or the reasons for my holding those views. Psychic inquiry demands a great deal more than cursory study. There are many mysteries of nature that men have looked upon as enigmas, until patience and research have solved them for them. Then they marvel how they could have been blind so long! Magnetism, spiritualism, and clairvoyance have all their mystical, as well as their explicable, side. It is only because they don't readily lend themselves to the comprehension of our material nature, that we try to scoff them into the limbo of absurdity and imposture."

"Ah," said Mrs. Jefferson. "Talking of clairvoyance, *that* I do believe in. I knew a coloured woman in America – the way that woman would tell you things– it was enough to make your flesh creep! She'd just go quietly off to sleep, and you might ask her anything you liked, and she'd tell you; and it was all as true as possible."

The princess met Julian Estcourt's eyes, and smiled strangely. Mrs. Jefferson caught the glance.

"Perhaps," she said, "you're a clairvoyant?"

"I used to be," she said, gravely "Perhaps my faculties have grown blunted, for want of use. They are far from being as keen as they were in India. However," and she smiled at the circle of faces, "I wonder if any of you would believe me if I told you what you were talking about at dinner time. First of all, you must remember your conversation could not have been betrayed to me by my friend, as he was not there, and that my rooms are on the opposite wing to the dining saloon. Well, you discussed different phases of spiritualism. This lady," she indicated Mrs. Masterman, "gave her experiences of imposture; you," looking at Mrs. Jefferson, "combated those experiences by your own, and this gentleman"—she smiled at the cynical individual, who was hovering on the outskirts of the circle—"silenced you all by reducing your theories to strong common-sense facts. Shall I quote his own words? After the rate people have been running after spiritual phenomena, they are absolutely refreshing. He said that it was an intensely humiliating idea to find oneself at the beck and call of any other human being when you imagined you had done with this life."

"Good gracious!" almost screamed Mrs. Jefferson, "but how on earth did you hear all this? It's positively alarming."

"Well," said the princess, still smiling at the pale and conscience-stricken faces, "you see I have a—faculty shall I call it?—that enables me to hear and see anything I am curious about, or interested in. I don't believe I could even explain how I do it; but it seems easy and natural enough to myself I only paid you a brief visit to-night, more that I might have a little bit of proof to give you that the powers I spoke of do exist, and are capable of being trained to almost any extent, if the motives for developing them are good. Have I convinced you?"

She rose as she spoke, and stood facing them in her beautiful indolent grace. She was garbed in some white soft stuff, which floated round her like a cloud, the wide hanging sleeves were lined with faint shell-like pink, and fell away from her bare lovely arms to the hem of her floating draperies. She looked like some goddess of mythology, rather than a living woman, and as Julian Estcourt gazed at her he felt a sudden thrill of awe.

Could that more than mortal beauty ever really be his—his in the common prose of possession that can never be disassociated with marriage—the prose that is to the delicate subtle beauty of love, what the rough touch is to the wings of the butterfly, the bloom of the grape?

For a moment the thought seemed like sacrilege. He could have fallen at her feet in a sudden adoration of the divine beauty and purity of embodied womanhood. "If ever she has lived before," he said in his heart, "it must have been as a vestal virgin, or a martyred saint. Where in the world is such another woman?

The voice of the cynical philosopher broke on his ear and disturbed his thoughts. "Madame, it is my humble opinion that you could convince us of anything you desired. Happy are those who have so charming a disciple to expound their doctrines, happier still the fortunate few to whom those doctrines are to be expounded by lips so lovely and a heart so wise."

Ere the circle had quite recovered from its astonishment at hearing a speech so flattering uttered by their surly Diogenes, they had parted to make way for the beautiful stranger,

and the last gleam of her snowy robes had
floated through the doorway, as a cloud melts
into the darkness of descending night.

There was a sort of long-drawn breath, a
feeling as of long tension suddenly set free,
a turning as if by one accord to one another.
Then—well, then all the tongues leaped into
action, and for the remainder of that evening,
like Thackeray's folk " At the Springs," they
talked, and they talked, *and they talked.*

CHAPTER X.

PREMONITION.

WHEN the Princess Zairoff was in the privacy
of her own boudoir, she turned to Colonel
Estcourt in a sudden appeal:

" Why did you make me go, Julian ? " she
said. " I knew I should only shock them.
I can't ever put up with that languid ignorant
curiosity."

" I think it will do them good to be
shocked," he said, with a smile. " Give them
something to think of beside their ailments.
And I had a special reason "—he went on with
a deeper note of tenderness in his voice—" I
do not wish you to shut yourself away as you
have been doing. You will grow morbid and
dissatisfied with life. I want you to take a
healthy interest in it once again."

She had thrown herself on a low cushioned
lounge before the bright wood fire. He took
a chair beside her. She seemed to lapse into
profound thought, and he watched her beautiful grave face with adoring eyes.

" I wish," she said suddenly, " one could live a free, simple, uncriticised life. Do you remember the old days among the wild hills ? . . . the cool grey dawns, the sharp sweet air . . . the long gallops over the rough roads by the rice fields . . . the strange temples, the songs of the snake-charmers ? Ah, we were happy then, Julian, happier than we ever realized."

" May we not be still happier ? " he said earnestly. " Life has a graver and a wider meaning, it is true, but that should only give us a deeper power of appreciation "

A strange smile touched her lips ; a smile of mystery, and of dreamy, unfathomable regret.

" We shall never be happier," she said, " than we were then. I have always felt that . . . yes, I know what you would ask. Did I love you then ? Yes, Julian, with all my heart and soul . . . and yet—and yet— I could have been nothing more to you than a sister, a friend. There was a purpose in my marriage."

She ceased speaking For a moment her eyes closed, her head sank back wearily on the soft cushions.

Presently she opened them, and met his anxious gaze. " No, I did not faint," she said. " But, why I know not, that sense of blankness and dizziness always comes over me when I speak on that subject There is something I wish, yet dread, to remember— but, just as I am on the point of grasping it, there is a blank."

" Do not speak of that time," he said

passionately. " I hate to think you were the wife of that man . . . it was sacrilege . . . you—my pure-souled goddess."

" He was a bad man," she said. " But, up to a certain point, I could always escape and defy him. He was a coward at heart, and he was afraid of me."

Then suddenly she stretched out her arm and touched his shoulder with a timid, caressing movement. " You need not be jealous of those years, my beloved," she said softly. " No man would, who knew them and valued them for what they were to me."

He sank on his knees, and folded his arms about her. " Ah, queen of mine," he said, " it is only natural that I should be jealous of the lightest touch, or look, or word, that were once another's privilege. Therein lies the only sting in my happiness——"

" Does not that prove it is of earth—earthly?" she said, as her deep mournful eyes looked back to his own. " I believe, Julian, it would be better, even now, if we were to part. I have always that dread upon my soul, that I am destined to bring you suffering—misfortune——"

" Bring me what you will," he interrupted passionately, " but do not speak of parting! Rather suffering and trial at your hands, oh, my life's love, than the greatest peace and prosperity from any other woman's !"

" I wish you loved me less," she said sadly. " But I am not forbidden to accept your love now; only, I have warned you, do not forget. And now "—she added suddenly : " Put me to sleep . . . it is so long, so long, since I have known real rest, such as you used to give me."

He rose slowly and stood beside her, as she nestled back amidst her cushions. A strange calm and chill seemed to fold him in its peace, and the throbbing fires of pain and longing died slowly out of vein and pulse. He laid one hand gently on the beautiful white brow; his eyes met hers, and the glance seemed like a command. The lids drooped, the long, soft lashes fell like a fringe on the delicate, flushed cheek. One ong, sobbing breath left her lips; then a beautiful serenity and calm seemed to enfold her. Like a statue, she lay there, motionless, stirless; lifeless, one would have thought, save for the faint regular breath that stole forth from the parted lips.

Julian Estcourt stood for a moment in perfect silence by her side. Then he moved away, and, drawing aside the *portières* which separated the boudoir from the adjoining room, he called softly to her maid. "Felicie," he said, "your mistress will sleep for two hours; see that she is not disturbed."

*   *   *   *   *

Once out in the cool night-air, Julian Estcourt gave the rein to thought and memory. The march of events had been rapid. It seemed difficult to realize that he really stood in the light of an accepted lover to the woman who, but the previous day, he deemed at the other end of the world . . . difficult to realize that she loved him—and had loved him through all the blank, desolate years of absence and suffering they had both endured.

Her warning came ever and again like a living voice across the fevered train of his thoughts. But he was no whit more inclined to listen to it here, in the calmness and soberness of solitude, than when her own lips had spoken it, and the charm of her own presence had swept away prudence and self-restraint.

"It may not be wise," he said in his heart, "but I have not the strength to deny myself the only happiness I have ever pictured as possible. It is not as if I had frittered away my life on other women—on mere sensual pleasures. From my boyhood up to the present hour her power has been the same—her charm for me the same, I love her. That says all, and yet not half enough. Human nature is weak. I had dreamt of another life —of a higher and nobler field of duty, apart from the selfish joys that are inseparable from mere human ties—but I can yield that dream up without a regret. I can turn back from the threshold I have crossed . . . May there not be a purpose in our meeting like this—in the prospect of our union? If the time has come to teach, and to speak out boldly what has long been veiled in mysticism and doubt, where could a teacher so eloquent be found, or one whose natural gifts and loveliness could make those teachings of so much weight? and I—I, too, can help and protect her. Our souls need not descend from the spiritual level they have attained—they may meet and touch, and yet expand in the duality of perfect love and perfect comprehension

It is a glorious thought," and he lifted his eyes to the starry heights, that to him held all the mystery of peopled worlds—and were no mere pin-pricks of light, created to illuminate *one.* "A beautiful thought—God grant it may be realized !"

But even as his eyes rested on the solemn splendour of the heavens—even as the human passions of the senses grew stilled beneath the loftier aspirations of the soul—even as that involuntary prayer sprang from heart to lips, some inner consciousness whispered like a warning voice—" *it cannot be.*"

He started as if that sound were audible. A cold and sudden terror swept over his body like a chilling wind. "Bah," he cried. "What a nervous fool I am ! Is this all my love has done for me—made me like a frightened child, starting at shadows ? "

He turned abruptly, and went within to seek his own room.

It was just midnight. Lights were being extinguished in the public rooms and corridors —silence and sleep were settling down upon the vast building.

Colonel Estcourt exchanged his evening clothes for the comfort of dressing-gown and slippers, and then threw himself into an easy chair before the fire which was blazing brightly and cheerfully in the grate.

It was the conventional hotel bedroom. A dressing-table stood in the window ; the bed, curtained and draped, looked inviting in its corner. A lamp stood on a small table littered with books and papers ; an array of pipes and cigar-holders were strewn carelessly on the marble mantelpiece. A sense of brightness and commonplace comfort permeated the atmosphere, and were sensibly soothing after the chill of the cool December night.

He took a cigar from his case and lit it, and threw himself back and smoked at his ease.

As he did so, he heard a clock in the distance strike the quarter after midnight, mechanically he counted the strokes. "She will wake now," he said, half aloud.

The sound of his voice startled himself in the stillness of the room. As its echoes died away he glanced nervously round. Then his face paled to the hues of death, his eyes dilated. Midway in the room a veiled misty figure seemed to float—transparent and yet distinct—and he saw its arm stretched out towards himself with a sudden impressive gesture.

He tossed the cigar into the grate, then bent his head as if in submission.

"Is it the summons—at last?" he said, faintly.

If answer there was, it was audible only to himself. To anyone looking on, it only seemed as if a sudden dreamy lassitude had overtaken him; his head sank back against the chair, his eyes closed, his face grew calm and peaceful, and, like a tired child, he fell asleep.

CHAPTER XI.

As Julian Estcourt's eyes closed, it seemed to him that with a sudden sharp spasm of pain he tore himself away from that sleeping sentient portion of humanity which was his representation, and then, without effort or consciousness of his own, he seemed floating swiftly along over a dark and misty space. A great sea tossed and moaned beneath him. He felt that someone was beside him, but he had no desire to question its personality. Now and then lights flashed through the dusky shadows which enveloped him, and as they flashed he saw vivid pictures of plains and cities and mountains.

Over one such city, bathed in the clear lucid flame of the full moon, he seemed to pause. He saw bridges, piles of buildings, dark flowing canals, a strange medley of streets, some broad and beautiful, others dark, narrow and pestilential, reeking with the fumes of dram-shops.

There was snow on the ground, sleighs were gliding swiftly to and fro. People spoke but seldom; an air of restraint, of fear, of rebellion impressed him, as the furtive glances and brief whispers became pregnant with meaning.

Gradually, as he moved through the

hurrying crowd, he was conscious of a name constantly on their lips. It was muttered by the voices of tipsy men reeling from their vile dens of intoxication, by the lips of painted women as they drew their furs around their tawdry finery, by the artisans with their pinched faces and hungry eyes, by all the classes to whom life is a bitter struggle with poverty and necessity.

To and fro he seemed to move, without haste, and yet with the rapidity of thought. In the magnificence of gilded saloons, in the snow-covered street, in the haunts of poverty and vice, always and always that one word was tossed to and fro in every accent of hate and opprobrium. And when in wonder he turned to the shape floating still beside him, and would have questioned the meaning of that word, it stayed the question on his lips with a mute gesture of silence.

Then, strange to say, he seemed to gather into his own consciousness a sense of deep implacable hatred. A hatred that thrilled the air as with poisoned breath, and beat in the pulses of living men to whom existence was brutalized by tyranny and vice. The sense of this awful murderous Hate, at last grew terrible as a burden, so fully and consciously did he recognise it, so clearly did he see of what it was capable, and so mysteriously did it seem to breathe about the very air through which he moved.

It filled the pulses of the night with a horror from which he shrank aghast, it stretched a blood-red hand over the white drifts of unsullied snow, it painted out the brilliant hues of luxury, and threw yet darker shadows over the sad homes of want and misery and crime.

And more and more he strained every nerve to catch the meaning of that word which was its embodiment, and again and again he failed.

Suddenly the scene changed. He was in a poor chamber, barely and miserably furnished. It lay in the centre of a pile of buildings facing a half-frozen canal It seemed to him that the building consisted of hosts of small tenements, all swarming with human life, but he had passed up the common stairway seemingly unnoticed, and entered this special room.

It was tenanted by two people. An old woman of some three-score years, with a thin worn face and grey hair banded over her hollow temples. She was thinly clad, and had an old tippet of yellow fur over her shoulders. She sat near the stove. Before her stood a young man in the dress of a Petersburgh student. They were talking low and earnestly. Again that word reached him, again the full sense of its meaning eluded his grasp.

Suddenly the comprehension of the scene became clear to him. He saw they were mother and son, that he was relating some incident to her with a suppressed enthusiasm that yet made itself audible in his deep, thrilling tone, and visible in the glow and sparkle of his eye.

" She is an angel," he said at last. " We do well to trust her—but what a risk, think of it, mother—five hundred lives, and only a few hours to decide their fate."

The woman's face grew white, her feeble limbs shivered as with an ague fit. "My son," she moaned, "my only one—and you, too, may be sacrificed. Oh, unhappy country, unhappy fate that makes it ours! But you are right. The Princess is an angel of goodness; she will save us. She has said it."

They both turned involuntarily towards a small image, before which a lamp burned. He saw them kneel hand in hand before it; then the room faded into darkness—he was in another place now.

A sense of luxury, of perfume, of dreamy warmth, and then he saw, opening before him in a vista of exquisite colour, a suite of softly lighted chambers. They seemed to glow like jewels, each perfect in the richness and loveliness of its setting, and at the farthest end of one of them a woman reclined on a couch of white furs She was wrapped in a loose gown of thick white silk, bordered also with snowy fur, and her lovely hair was unbound, and fell in a long trail of dusky splendour over the colourless purity of her surroundings.

Her eyes were wide open, and full of a fear that was almost horror, and, as if to account for it, he seemed suddenly to hear, coming through the fragrant stillness of those virginal chambers, the dull heavy step of a man. She raised herself on one lovely bare arm, her hand went to her heart, then slowly her eyes were upraised as if in some dumb prayer for strength. A strange frozen calm came over the perfect features. The face looked as if carved in marble.

Nearer and nearer came the heavy step, reeling and uncertain now, yet stumbling with drunken obstinacy towards some goal to which the leaden senses pointed their brutal desires.

Up to this time, Julian Estcourt had only been conscious of a passive blind submission to the force controlling him; but now power seemed to thrill him, desire seemed struggling to life, the will awakened from its lethargy, and a god-like strength and force seemed to spring into life, held in check but for a moment, as the increased vigilance of sense bade him watch yet a little longer.

With breath reeking of drink, with blood-shot eyes and reeling step, the satyr entered. Yet so great was the spell and charm of that womanly purity and dauntless pride, that even lust and tyranny sank abashed on the threshold, and a certain shame and hesitance were visible in the flushed face and bloodshot eyes."

"Why are you here?" asked the woman calmly. "Have you mistaken your way?"

"No,"—and the intruder advanced with sudden boldness. "I have come to ask if you are still of the same mind—still intent on destroying your *friends*." His laugh rang out mockingly. "Fine friends truly for a Princess Zairoff. I gave you till to-night—come, which is to be sacrificed—your womanly scruples, or the five hundred lives you have fooled into security?"

Then she sprang to her feet, a statue no longer, but a living, passionate woman.

"I have borne enough," she cried. "Beware how you tempt the power that has been strong enough to keep me from you all these years. Beware, too, how, once again, you stain your soul with innocent blood. Thousands of voices are crying against you even now. Thousands of years of suffering on your part will not avail to buy you peace in the future. I have prayed for these unfortunates, I have begged their lives at your hands on my very knees. Do not tempt me too far. I say again—you do not know what it is you do."

He laughed brutally. "I know," he said, "that you shall pay for their lives, or sacrifice them. I have waited long enough. I am sick of hearing men rave about your beauty, and feeling that that beauty is no more to me than if I were a beggar at my own gates."

"Do you forget," she said solemnly, "the compact we made? I am not at any man's choice, or disposal. My life has a mission to accomplish, and you, with all your brutal desires and evil passions, cannot turn that life from its destined purpose. Do not forget the warnings you have already received."

So beautiful she looked, standing there in her floating, snowy draperies, with her solemn, mysterious eyes fixed upon that sullen, lowering face. Beautiful and mysterious as some vestal priestess defending the secrets of her Order. But that beauty, for once, seemed less to subjugate than to inflame the evil desires of that lower nature to which it was bound.

"I will listen no more to vague threats,"

he said fiercely. "I have paid a heavy enough price for you. I mean to enjoy my purchase. See, here is the list—they are fairly trapped—a word from you and they are safe—these impatient fools. Keep silence —and the knout, the mines, the slow torturing death of Siberia, awaits them all. Now, once again—your answer?"

He drew nearer—his eyes aflame—his arms outstretched.

Then a change, wild and fearful, as that of the tropical tornado to a southern landscape, swept over that lovely form. Her eyes flashed, her figure seemed to dilate. Slowly she raised her arm and stretched it towards that brutal ravisher. . .

*   *   *   *   *

Struggling, panting, tearing, as it were, against a power that bade him hearken to that terrible answer, Julian Estcourt cried or seemed to cry aloud in an agony of entreaty.

Then a rushing noise as of an unloosed torrent was in his ears; a dull, confused pain beat like clanging hammers in his brain.

His eyes opened and he found himself, bathed in the cold sweat of more than mortal terror, lying face downwards on the floor of his own bedroom.

*   *   *   *   *

In a blind, dazed fashion he struggled to his feet and rushed to the window and let the cool night air blow over his face. Every limb was trembling, he could not think with any clearness.

In some dim, unconscious fashion he groped for his watch, and found it, and looked at the time. A quarter-past one. Only an hour had passed—an hour—and he felt as if centuries had swept over his head in the vivid horrors of that awful dream.

"But it was only a dream," he cried aloud, drawing in deep panting breaths of the pine-scented air. "Oh! thank God. Thank God, it was only a dream!" . . . .

And he sank on his knees and sobbed like a child in the star-lit solitude of the night.

CHAPTER XII.

EFFECTS.

THE next day, when Colonel Estcourt sent to know if the Princess Zairoff would receive him, he was informed she was ill, and could see no one.

Feeling strangely disinclined for mere ordinary society, he ordered his horse to be brought round and spent the greater portion of the day in long, fierce gallops over the miles of stretching sand that framed in the bay.

The sky was chill and grey; a cold wind blew from the sea and dashed the salt foam in his face as the waves swept stormily in. But the dull sky and the stormy sea suited his mood, and seemed to string up the relaxed tension of his nerves.

"Nature is man's best physician after all," he said to himself, reining in his beautiful Arab at last, and baring his brow to the fresh breeze. "Even as she is his best

friend.   Only we don't believe it.   We live
in the world and follow the ways of the
world, until our faculties are blunted, our
natures demoralized, our tastes vitiated, our
energies enfeebled.   How many lands I have
travelled over, how many cities I have seen,
and yet I verily believe that the wild Sioux
in his prairies, and the wandering Bedouin
of the desert, have more of real manhood
than we   Yes; and get more real enjoyment
out of life."

It was quite dusk before he reached the
hotel.   The country was all new and strange
to him, and he had missed his way more than
once.   But though he was tired, and stiff,
and hungry, he felt that his mental energies
were braced, his mind at ease, and the
disturbing and torturing memories of the
previous night no longer tormented him.

At dinner he sat next to Mrs. Ray
Jefferson, who was radiant and voluble
as ever.

She had a great deal to say about the
Princess, who, it appeared, had again spent
the morning in the Baths.

" She looked ill," said the little American.
" Awfully white and languid.   I asked her if
she had seen a ghost.   There was something
scared and strange about her.   I surmise it's
nerves.   It was odd, too," and she lowered
her voice as if taking the Colonel into a
special confidence.   " But she went off to
sleep in the hot room.   Nothing could waken
her.   I got rather frightened."

His face looked disturbed.   " To sleep?" he
said.   " That is rather unusual, is it not?"

"Oh, plenty of us go to sleep in the cooling-room," said Mrs. Jefferson, " but I never saw anyone do it in any of the others. She was talking to me, and then quite suddenly she said 'I feel sleepy. Please do not speak. I shall wake in a quarter of an hour.' And so she did."

" You did not try to waken her, I suppose?" asked Colonel Estcourt anxiously.

" Well, I did, but it was no use, so I let her be. I saw she was all right, because she breathed naturally, and her heart beat quite regularly. Still, it seemed odd. I asked her maid afterwards about it. She's a pretty little Frenchwoman, and always waits in the cooling-room for her mistress. But she didn't seem to think anything of it. She said she very often does that, and it is best not to try and waken her. I must say she seemed much better afterwards. Brighter and more alert. What a lovely creature she is!" she added enthusiastically. " I suppose you know you're the most envied person in the hotel at this present moment?"

He smiled, but his face still looked anxious and disturbed.

" Because I have the privilege of being her friend?" he said. " Well, I am not going to deny that it *is* a privilege—a most enviable one."

" I should think," said Mrs. Jefferson meaningly, " it is also one that has its dangers."

The calm grey eyes met her sharp inquisitive glance, but were utterly unrevealing.

" I will not affect to misunderstand you,"

he said, " but there are men who covet danger
for its own sake. They may seem foolhardy,
but they are only accountable to themselves
for the risks they run."

"Well," said Mrs. Jefferson warmly, "I'm
only a woman, and yet if it's possible to fall
in love with one of my own sex, I've done it.
She's perfectly charmed me. I can't get her
out of my head for a single moment. It's not
only her wonderful beauty, but her mind. As
for our poet," she added, laughing, "he's
quite gone He's done nothing all day but
moon about under the pine trees. Writing
sonnets, I guess, and hoping to catch a
glimpse of her. All useless—she's not left the
hotel to-day, and I suppose she'll not favour
us to night."

Colonel Estcourt was silent. Conversation
was more or less general, but it sounded
vague and unmeaning to him. He heard a
voice on his left holding forth with energy,
but he did not heed it until Mrs. Jefferson
touched his arm and whispered an entreaty.

"Do listen," she said, "it's Diogenes. Isn't
he coming out ? I surmise it's *her* influence.
You remember last night ? "

"An atheist," said the dogmatic voice of the
individual who had given that common-sense
view of spiritualism the previous evening,
" must be a fool of the most complete type.
Because he doubts what *men* teach of God,
is no reason for doubting the existence *of* God.
I grant that the Reverend John Smith, with
his high-falutin' trappings of Ritualism on one
side, and the Reverend Josiah Stiggins, with
his coarse and commonplace familiarity with

the Almighty (whose personality he has the effrontery to expound as if he were discussing the characteristics of an ordinary mortal), on the other, are enough to drive hundreds of people out of the pale of Christianity, and force them to take refuge in defiance and opposition. But, all the same, the expectation of another life is a rooted belief in the minds of all men, quite apart from religion. Even the savage has it. If we call it human nature to eat, drink, fight, love, or desire, it must also be human nature that gives universal assent to this idea of an after existence. The fact of finding it in all races is but a proof that Man is the creation of a Power that intends him for a far wider range of existence than he sees before him. There are many things affirmed by man's consciousness that he cannot really or logically explain. Yet it is a narrow reasoning that bids us reject the inexplicable."

"Yet you reject spiritualism," said Mrs. Jefferson quickly.

"Not at all, my dear madam. I only reject the humiliating and degrading trickery that is its sensational form. I only repeat what I said yesterday, that no lofty or educated mind could do anything but resent the idea of being subjugated to a mere material will, and being forced by that will to perform conjuring tricks in order that a small portion of the civilized world should gape, and gaze, and cry out 'How wonderful!' To deny that spirits exist, aye and work, would be to deny the very crudest faith in Christianity."

"There is no doubt," said Colonel Estcourt, "that everything *is* explicable, but we must wait for the growth and development of our higher natures before we can comprehend half the mysteries of the higher life. The great fault of the materialist and the scientist is, that they would fain bring everything down to the level of their *present* comprehension, instead of patiently waiting the completion of their future spiritual forces. It is quite evident that we are not meant to attain our full mental stature on the earth plane, or what would be left to achieve in the countless ages of immortality? Man believes in immortality and yet seems to contemplate it as a state of stagnation and quiescence. Why he believes in it he cannot fully explain. It is, as you said before, a consciousness given to the races of humanity, but no more capable of commonplace analysis than time, or space, or thought."

"The beautiful is as the cloud that floats in radiant space," murmured the poet. "The very vagueness of form permits the eye to clothe it in the loveliest tints of Fancy."

"Now that's what I call rational," murmured Mrs. Jefferson in Colonel Estcourt's ear. "Do you think he knows what he means. I guess he don't. . . . Gracious!'

She started, and suddenly grasped his arm. "Look," she said, "there's the princess in the doorway. Is she coming in? No! She's moving away. I believe she's going into the drawing-room after all. Did you see her?"

"No," said Colonel Estcourt. "Are you sure it was the princess?"

His face looked strangely pale She saw that his hand trembled as he laid down his knife on the plate before him."

"Sure?" exclaimed Mrs. Jefferson, with asperity. "Of course I'm sure! It's not easy to mistake *her*, I fancy. I can't think why you didn't catch sight of her. She just looked in as she passed, I suppose."

"No doubt," he said. But the gravity and uneasiness of his face deepened.

Just then one of the waiters paused beside Mrs. Jefferson's chair. She turned eagerly to him. "Watson," she said, "just oblige me by going to the drawing-room and finding out if Madame Zairoff is there. I guess," she added laughingly to Colonel Estcourt, "that I'm not going to waste my time over thirteen courses if she is."

Still he did not speak, and his unusual pallor and gravity began to affect the lively little American woman. She helped herself to truffled pheasant, and became absorbed in gastronomical duties.

Two or three minutes passed, when the man who had gone on her errand returned. She glanced eagerly up.

"Madame Zairoff is not in the drawing-room," he said in a low voice. "I met her maid on the stair-case, and she says that madame is not well enough to leave her apartments this evening."

"But, good gracious me," began Mrs. Jefferson, with angry impatience. "I saw——"

"Hush," said Colonel Estcourt in a low, impressive voice. "Oblige me by saying nothing about it. Remember, I too was looking in the same direction, yet I saw —nothing."

Mrs. Jefferson dropped her knife and fork and stared at him.

"Now, Colonel," she said, "am I in my senses, or am I not? I've only had iced water to drink. I believe I'm a commonplace person eating a commonplace, though very excellent, dinner. Nothing's been playing tricks with my nerves I can swear, and I do assure you that the Princess Zairoff stood there in that doorway and looked in here, not five minutes ago. Why, I'll even tell you the gown she had on. It was thick white silk and had a border of soft-looking white fur. There!" she added triumphantly. "You may go up to her rooms after dinner, and if she hasn't got that gown on, and if she didn't come by that doorway—well—I'll say I've gone stark staring mad! That's so!"

CHAPTER XIII.

A PROMISE.

JUST as the ladies had left the dining-room, a note was put into Colonel Estcourt's hand.

He opened it and read the two brief lines it contained. "I will see you in my boudoir when you have finished dinner."

He pushed aside the glass he had just filled and left the table at once.

He knocked at the door of her room, and the low, sweet voice that bade him enter, thrilled his heart with its accustomed sorcery.

He opened the door, but as he stepped across the threshold. he suddenly paused, and for a moment it seemed to him that his heart ceased to beat. Was it only chance that reproduced the dream-scene of the previous night, for the suite of rooms were thrown open, and through the delicate amber tints of the satin hangings gleamed the faint rose-hue of lamp-light, paling into opal in the farthest chamber but giving to all the soft and glowing colouring he remembered so well. Swiftly as his eyes took in the picture, they seemed also to take in the lovely figure reclining among soft snowy furs, robed in colourless silk bordered with the same fur.

She raised herself on her arm as he approached. "I have not treated you well to-day, Julian," she said. "But I have been ill—nervous—disturbed. I slept badly, and had terrible dreams. You must forgive me."

He bent over the extended hand and touched it with his lips.

"You are cold," she said. "What is the matter?"

"I too, had a terrible dream," he said. "I suppose the effects are still upon me." Then he looked calmly and fixedly at her.

"You were downstairs a few moments ago," he said. "Why?"

She looked surprised. "Did you see me?" she asked.

He shook his head. "No," he said. "It was your American friend."

Her face grew thoughtful. "Then the power *is* coming back," she said. "I wonder why."

He seated himself beside her. "Of course," he said, "it was not really yourself?"

"I have not left this couch for three nours," she said. "All the same, I wanted to have a peep at you all."

"I hope you will not exercise that power too frequently," he said. "You know I never liked it."

"I know," she said, smiling up at his grave face, "that you were always afraid I should not come back from my flights, but I always do. *They* send me—very much against my will—still, I must obey."

She sighed. Then after a moment she put out her hand with a caressing little gesture. "What was your terrible dream?" she said. "I see it is troubling you still. You are *distrait* and absent. Tell me."

He touched the white hand with his lips.

"I would rather not," he said, "because you were concerned in it, and it seemed as if you were trying to reveal something or show me something that I dreaded to see. It was in fighting against seeing it that I awoke."

She started from her reclining position and fixed her eyes on his face "Julian," she cried, in a sudden breathless way, "was it —was it?—No—" She broke off and wrung her hands helplessly. "It has escaped me again. I *cannot* remember. Oh, that I could! It tortures me so. Julian"—and she looked at him appealingly. "*You* must help me— you must bring it back. I will not wed you till that mystery is solved. Something warns me against it."

"My dearest," he said soothingly, "do not excite yourself in this fashion. It can make no difference to me that there should be mystery or tragedy in your past life. Have I not always loved you? Have we not chosen the same path in life, only now we shall tread it side by side, not one far in advance of the other? The infinite delight of that companionship shall not be marred by any memories of the past. If I am content to let it rest, surely you may be."

She drew herself away. Her deep strange eyes looked coldly and yet mournfully back to his yearning gaze.

"You were never a coward, Julian," she said. "What is it you fear now?"

He threw himself on his knees by her side and buried his face in the soft white furs. She saw that he was trembling greatly. "I cannot tell," he said hoarsely. "Would to God that I could! But if you should change, if you should repent—Oh! to lose your love now would kill me!"

She laid her hand on his bowed head. "Rest assured you shall not lose *that*," she said in her low thrilling voice. "No, Julian, that is not the danger—it threatens me, not you. There will be no change on my part, not so far as my love is concerned. Will that assurance satisfy you?"

"You need not ask that, beloved? But why disturb our peace? If I am content——"

"There must be no secret between your soul and mine," she said solemnly. "For what, think you, is your power granted, but that I may answer to it, that I may lead you on the road—and that you, for me, may throw open the portals?"

"In the future," he said eagerly, "I am content to do your will. But not now—not to draw the veil from our buried miseries. Let them be as dead things—out of sight and mind."

"You know," she said, "that nothing dies —not a life, or an act, or a thought. You may put the past out of sight, but it lives still—lives in its hidden crimes, its secret sins, its evil and its good—lives to haunt and shape our future, let that future dream as it will of forgetfulness."

He rose from his knees, his face was still pale, but his eyes glowed like living fire.

"When will you wed me, Estarah?" he asked, abruptly.

The soft colour flushed her cheek. Her eyes drooped.

"My heart is yours," she said. "My life lives but in the shadow of your own. Why should I withhold—this poor gift?"

She placed her hand in his, and let him draw her to his heart. "I will wed you when you will," she said, "but only if you yield to my condition. It is an easy one, Julian. Why do you fear?"

Ah—why? He could not answer that question to his own heart, much less to hers. He could not paint the shuddering horror which had forced him to veil his eyes and shrink aghast from that last scene in his Dream.

Yet when he looked down on her in her pure womanly beauty, and felt the clinging tenderness of her arms, and knew that among all the world of men who had worshipped and wooed her, he alone had kept his place and awakened a response of tenderness, he felt his heart thrill and glow with sudden strength and pride.

"It shall be as you wish," he said. "On the night that heralds our bridal morn, I promise, if my power be still the same, that I will do your bidding."

She lifted her face. It was radiant with a strange mysterious joy. "At last," she said, brokenly—"at last I shall know. Every page of my life will be clear. Heart to heart, soul to soul, so we shall stand, oh, beloved! You and I, with senses purified, with no secret unshared, with spirits un‑fettered and souls at rest, so shall we greet our bridal morn. For this did I brave the ordeal, for this have I faced almost the bitter‑ness of death—but the trial is almost over—the goal is almost reached. Go, now, my life's beloved, lest indeed my heart should break beneath its weight of joy! Go; but fear not. I am yours for ever in the life we know, and in the deep Unknown beyond I shall claim you still!"

CHAPTER XIV.

THE DREAM INTERPRETED.

FOR some days no one in the hotel saw the Princess Zairoff. But her influence seemed to have left a distinct impression, judging from the run on Buddhist literature at the different circulating libraries of the town. The " Occult World," " Isis Unveiled," and " Esoteric Buddhism " were in great demand; so were various works on Mesmerism, Clairvoyance, and Occult Science.

The poet plunged into " Zanoni," which he had read in the days of 'his boyhood as one reads a fairy-tale, and he and Mrs. Ray Jefferson, being the greatest enthusiasts, held long and learned and quite unintelligible discussions over these mysterious subjects, with a view to being able to hold their own with the beautiful proselytiser when she should deign to come amongst them all once more.

The weather had changed, and kept the invalids indoors, so there was plenty of time for " serious reading," as Mrs. Jefferson called it.

They took to calling the Princess " the Eastern mystery," and were quite certain that she must be gifted with abnormal powers. Mrs. Jefferson related the story of her appearance in the doorway, her belief in it having long since been substantiated by Colonel Estcourt's reluctant admission that the Princess was certainly attired in a white silk gown, bordered and trimmed with white fur, when he went up to her rooms that evening.

Mrs. Masterman alone held out, and scoffed audibly at the mystic literature, and what she called the " insane jabber " that went on in the drawing-room every evening.

" Psychic phenomena, indeed !" the worthy lady would snort. " Don't talk to me about such rubbish! It's just as bad as the mediums and the slate writers."

"Dear madam," pleaded the gentle voice of the enamoured poet, "do not, I pray you, confound these great mysteries with the strain of Human Error running through their attempted explanation—an explanation only intended to bring them down to the level of our material understandings. Let me persuade you to read that most exquisite poem ' The Light of Asia.' "

"Light of your grandmother!" exclaimed Mrs Masterman with sublime contempt.

"I fear," lamented the poet, "it never was granted to her. She lived in a benighted age. She had not our privileges."

"And a very good thing too!" said the purple-visaged dowager wrathfully. " Privileges indeed! Fine privileges, if honest, sober-minded Christians are to learn the way to Heaven from heathens and idolaters. You are all just as bad as those people St. Paul speaks of, who were always running after some new thing. I'm happy to say *my* Bible and *my* Church are good enough for me. I don't want a new religion at my time of life."

" The teachers in the Church are so very frequently our intellectual inferiors," murmured the poet, " that they only excite commiseration, or amusement."

"Well, I suppose they know their business," snapped Mrs. Masterman, "I'm sure no man would go into the Church if he didn't feel a call, and the fact of his doing so and taking up that life should be enough to

prevent any right-minded person from ridicul
ing mere human frailties of voice and manner
and appearance "

"Unfortunately," murmured the poet, "I
have been at college with several embryo
parsons. But to the best of my recollection
the only 'special' call they had for the office
was the call of some earthly relative or friend
who had a comfortable living at his disposal.
It seems to me—I may be wrong, of course
—but it really does seem to me that we
have quite reversed the old order of religious
ministration. At first every worldly consideration, even the necessaries of life, were given
up by those who undertook the office. Now,
the office is only undertaken *for* the worldly
considerations, and the necessities of life——"

"Oh," cried Mrs. Masterman, losing her
temper, which even at the best of times was
exceedingly hard to keep. "You go off,
young man, to your 'Lights of Asia,' and all
your other idolatrous rubbish. The truth is
this foreign woman has bewitched you all,
and will end in making you heathens like herself Thank goodness I've too much sense to
listen to her. It's my belief she'll turn out a
murderess, or a fire worshipper, or something
of that sort before we've seen the last of her.
I don't like mysterious persons! If she
hadn't had big eyes, and a straight nose, and
a figure like those Venuses and creatures who
hold the lamps in the corridors, no one here
would have troubled their heads about her!"

And she swept away contemptuously,
leaving the poet utterly aghast at her last in-
dignant speech. He repeated it to Mrs. Ray

Jefferson, who was reclining in a rocking-chair, endeavouring to comprehend "The Light of Asia." The endeavour, however, was not very successful, and she hailed the approach of the poet with delight. His account of the conversation filled her with wrath and indignation. The feelings might have been partially due to Mrs. Masterman's remembered snubs on the matter of "feet," and " suppressed gout," at the Turkish Bath. They certainly rose strongly to the occasion, and, with the help of sundry powerful Americanisms, gave a very fair display of vituperative eloquence.

The poet was more and more convinced that there was only one perfect woman in the world, and that was the beautiful creature whom he had apostrophised in sonnets as

" Mysterious Mystery, whose bright sad eyes,
Wild as the roe, and deep with undreamt dreams."

&c., &c.

So he listened and sighed, and in a low and plaintive voice, significant of hidden woe and much " soul suffering," to quote from another effusion, he read to her fragments of the " Light of Asia," which she could not in the least comprehend, but which she bluntly criticised as "not half bad to listen to if you felt drowsy."

"Oh, but I do wish the Princess would come down," she said at last in the intervals of a "selection." "I've such hundreds of questions to ask her. Seems to me she dropped the seed in pretty fruitful soil the other night, for we're all just 'gone' on occultism. Only we don't know anything about it. Ah, there's Colonel Estcourt, I'll ask him if it's possible to have her down this evening. I don't mind which body she comes in: the Astral or the ordinary. In fact, I think I should prefer the former. Colonel!" she called out, raising her voice. "Come here, I want to speak to you."

She put her request to him as he obeyed her summons, and put it with an earnestness and fervour that showed it was sincere, and not the formula of idle curiosity.

"I don't know," he said, "if it will be possible, but, if the princess consents, I will arrange that two or three of you shall have an opportunity of witnessing how really marvellous her powers are. She never makes a display or show of them, for reasons which you cannot yet understand, but, if she consents, I should like you, Mrs. Jefferson, and my young friend here (smiling at the poet's excited face), and one or two other people interested in the matter, to come up to her boudoir this evening. I will just send up a note and ask."

"I could just worship you, Colonel," cried the little American, ecstatically. "It's real good of you to offer such a glorious treat to us"

"Do not thank me yet," he said, smiling; "you do not know whether you will be received."

At the same moment there came a sound in the air above their heads—soft, clear, vibrating—like the faint echo of a silver bell.

Mrs. Jefferson started, the poet turned pale. Colonel Estcourt looked at them gravely

"It is the answer," he said. "You may come. She will receive us. Who else do you wish to invite?"

"Oh, my husband, if I may," cried Mrs. Jefferson, eagerly, "and Diogenes—he's so solid and sensible. His imagination never plays tricks with him."

"Very well," said Colonel Estcourt, "bring them also."

* * * * *

The Princess Zairoff was seated in her boudoir reading, as the party filed in, headed by Colonel Estcourt.

She rose and greeted them with the same sweet and gracious manner that had so charmed Mrs. Jefferson.

"I know why you are here," she said, as the little American burst into vivacious explanations. "I am quite ready to do anything Julian wishes. You know—or, perhaps, you do not know—that he trained my *clairvoyante* faculties long ago. They are natural to me, I suppose; but you do not require to be told that even natural gifts are capable of training and improving to almost any extent." She turned to Mrs. Jefferson. "You have some power," she said, "you saw me the other night. No one else did."

Mrs. Jefferson looked highly gratified. "Oh, Madame Zairoff," she cried, "I'd give up everything in the world to have your wonderful gifts."

"Even Worth's gowns?" said the princess, smiling. "What about the pleasant vanities we talked so much about?"

"Oh, bother the vanities. I've found out

life can be much more interesting than when it's merely frivolous," said the American, heartily. "Is there anything I *could* do to become an occultist?"

Colonel Estcourt laughed outright.

"My dear Mrs. Jefferson," he said, "the life is not by any means easy, or gratifying. I think you had better consider it carefully, and weigh it well in the balance with the 'creations' of Worth, and the magnificence of your diamonds, for somehow the two things won't pull together, and you haven't even learnt the A B C of occult science yet."

"No," she said, seating herself, "I suppose not. Well, please begin my lesson."

"This will not be a lesson," he said, gravely, "only an illustration. May I ask you all to be seated?"

They took various chairs and seats, and the princess threw herself on the couch, nestling back among her favourite white bear-skins, with a smile on her lips.

Colonel Estcourt removed a rose-shaded lamp from the stand, and placed it behind her, so that the light should not shine directly into her eyes. They were all watching her intently in the full expectation of something to be done or said that was mysterious and awe-inspiring. Colonel Estcourt then seated himself on a chair opposite the couch. For a moment their eyes met and lingered in the gaze, then hers closed softly, and she seemed to sleep as peacefully and gently as a child in its cradle.

No one spoke. Suddenly a voice broke the stillness—clear, sweet, and sonorous—the voice of the sleeper, though her lips scarcely moved, nor did the placid expression of her face change.

" What you desire to know is the storied wisdom of past ages, the fruits of the deepest and most earnest research of which human minds are capable. These fruits have only been gathered after long and painful study, after severe training of every spiritual faculty, and the repression of all lower material inclinations and desires. There is but one among all who listen to me now, capable of undertaking such study, or undergoing such an ordeal. The day is at hand when he may choose it, if he will. They who bid me speak now, are willing that you should learn some lesson to benefit yourselves, and your fellow men. They say to you, oh Poet, ' Perfect those gifts of your higher nature—yet be not of them vainglorious, since, humanly speaking, they are not yours, but lent for a purpose, and the brief space of earth-life. Look upon every beautiful thought, every gift of expression, as the direction of One who has dowered you with the possibility of opening other eyes to the beauty, and other minds to the understanding of such expression. Remember there is a great truth in your favourite lines that *Karma* is ' the total of a soul.' ' The things it did, the thoughts it had, the Self it wove, with woof of viewless time, crossed on the warp invisible of acts.'

" There is another listener here—one who has wrestled with the secrets of Nature. To him I say, ' Be not over vain of the triumph gained by simple accident of discovery. Turn that discovery to better uses than the mere amassing of wealth. Let the poor, the sick,⸱ the needy, gain health and happiness from your hands, and let their voices bless you for good wrought amongst them. For nothing is so pitiful and so abhorrent, as the worship of wealth, and the selfishness that eats like a corroding poison into the purer metal of the rich man's nature. Your wealth will only bring you happiness in so far as you use it to benefit others less fortunate though equally deserving. It is given you as a trial, not as a reward.' . . . To you, oh Cynic, this message have I also: 'Your eyes see but through a veil of dulled and vainglorious senses. Some truths you have learned, but in the passage through your mind they take the colour and shape of a distorted and embittered fancy. You have a work to do, and influence to do it; but your *will* must become humble, and then you will learn the sweets of true knowledge, and be able to disseminate truth and wisdom. Now you absorb it into your own mind, for your own satisfaction, and for the poor triumph of discouraging those of lower mental stature, and of natures lighter and grosser than your own. To the true Prophet and the true Philosopher, he himself is insignificant before the great truths he has learnt, and his personal identity willingly sinks into obscurity, so only that these truths may live.'"

For a moment she ceased, and the different faces looked curiously uncomfortable and startled at so keen a vivisection of their inner natures. Mrs. Ray Jefferson, however, feeling that she had been left out in the cold, and anxious for a special message to herself, broke the spell of silence.

"Have you nothing to say to me, Princess?" she asked beseechingly.

Then the beautiful head moved restlessly to and fro, and the face grew less placid and child-like. She began to speak, but now the words came in quick disjointed fragments. "They are standing beside you," she said. "I must go. You may come with us, but not Julian. Keep Julian away .... keep Julian away ——"

"What does she mean?" cried Mrs. Jefferson, turning pale. "And—oh gracious!" she cried to her husband, "look at Colonel Estcourt. Is he going to faint?"

All eyes turned on the Colonel. He lay back on his chair white and gasping. "My God," he cried in a stifled voice. "My power is gone. I can't hold her. I can't keep her back."

"She is speaking again," cried Mrs. Jefferson, in low, terrified accents. "Oh, I don't half like this. I wish we had never come."

Then a great awe and stillness fell upon them, and, despite their terror and their dread, every ear strained to catch the quick disjointed words that fell from those strange lips.

"I am there. .... How still the streets are, and the snow—how fast it falls. How they crowd round the palace gate to-night Stay the horses, Ivan, I will speak. .... Do not fear, my friends, your lives are safe. I promise it. ... What is this? My rooms? How lonely they seem to-night. 'Alone?'

Yes, I am always alone.   No lover's step has
ever echoed through this cloistered silence.
Alone and sad.   Ah! how I have suffered
here. . . . . What do they say?   It will be
over soon, it will be over—soon.   One more
battle . to win.   Let me summon all my
courage now.   I have faced ordeals before.
I have forgotten woman's fears, and laid
aside woman's scruples.   Am I not pure?
Am I not brave?   Yet why do I tremble?
. . . . One weakness is still unconquered, one
human love burns true and deep and steadfast
in my heart.   I cannot cast it out.   I *will* not;
not even at your bidding; not even to make
my task easier.

"A step in the silence. . . . . Who dares
to cross my chambers?   Courage, my heart.
There on the threshold stand my White Guard.
Why should I fear? . . . .   Courage!
courage——"

Like one carved in stone Julian Estcourt
sat and listened.   The dumb misery of a terrible
expectance held every faculty in its iron
grasp.   Was his dread to be realised? . . . .
It seemed so, for all control was gone; a
higher power had seized the reins.   She had
escaped him, and an awful horror was upon
him lest he, in his folly and shortsightedness,
had assembled these people here only to be
witnesses of the degradation of the peerless
creature he had so worshipped and so loved.

Spell-bound they sat and listened.   The
rose-light from the lamps falling upon their
white, set faces, and the quivering tension of
their silent lips.

The voice of the sleeper went ruthlessly on.

Scene for scene, word for word, Julian Estcourt lived over again through the wild dread and horror of his Dream. Scene for scene, word for word, those wondering startled listeners saw it reproduced, though to them it was scarce intelligible.

At last, she reached the point where his endurance had snapped beneath the strain of terror, but now his every force was numbed—his will seemed paralyzed. One feeble helpless effort he made to lock those lips into silence, to chain back the self-betrayal of that unconscious speech. But love had made him weak, and passion had stifled the acute, unerring faculties that once had bent her to his will.

He was powerless. He could only sit there dumbly—stupidly—listening for what he felt was sure as the death stroke of the headsman to his doomed victim. Again she spoke.

"The steps approach — yet what is this? *They* are no longer on the threshold. I am alone—alone—yet what new power is mine! My brain seems to dilate! . . . . Space can scarce confine me! All fear has gone! . . . . And it is thus you would have me yield to your brutal force, your drunken, degraded senses! . . . . Back, rash intruder, touch me not if you value life!" . . . .

Then, while still they gazed and listened, the beautiful figure rose slowly from its nest of snowy furs; rose and stood in its wonderful, indolent, voluptuous grace, upright before those dazed and awe-struck eyes.

But a change came over the quiet beauty

of the face. It seemed as if some hidden flame had sprung to life and flashed and quivered in the wide-opened eyes and convulsed features. · They saw a shiver, such as shakes the sea before the blast of the coming tempest, bend and sway the perfect form . . .

Once, twice, her lips opened, but no words came. At last she seemed to force the channels of speech, but the low sweet music of her voice was harsh and jangled with passion.

"My answer? . . . . Take it, ravisher and murderer of innocence and youth! Die! in your crimes—Die!" . . . .

She stretched out her arm. There came a hoarse cry, a crash, a heavy fall. Julian Estcourt lay upon the floor, white and senseless as the dead.

CHAPTER XV.

EXPIATION.

A SEVERE attack of her "suppressed" enemy, and a nervous headache, the result of the shock of the previous evening, had driven Mrs. Ray Jefferson to the Turkish bath as early as ten o'clock the morning after that strange exhibition of Clairvoyance.

She had the rooms all to herself, and as she leant back in her comfortable chair and dabbled her pretty bare feet in warm water, she reflected in a troubled and disjointed fashion over all that had occurred since that eventful morning when the beautiful "mystery" had appeared before her standing in that curtained archway, which indeed looked a prosaic enough portal, and not by any means the sort of threshold for the development of occult science, or psychical marvels.

"She's completely unsettled me," she murmured plaintively. "How I wish I had never gone to her rooms last night. And that poor Colonel Estcourt—I wonder if he'll ever recover—they say he's never moved nor spoken since they took him away last night. I wonder what she really meant, and if she did kill that man she spoke of. I don't think it's possible. I expect she only *willed* it, and that's not murder. Ugh!" and she shuddered even in the warmth of the hot room where she had selected to go first. "If the story leaks out—though I hope to goodness it won't—how delighted that horrid Mrs. Masterman will be. She never liked her. Well I'm——if that isn't the princess herself coming in! Her trance doesn't seem to have hurt her."

Slowly and languidly through the open doorway, the beautiful figure swept in and up to the smaller chamber where sat the little American.

As Mrs. Ray Jefferson looked at her, she became conscious of some subtle intangible change that had shadowed, as it were, the marvellous beauty of her face and form. Her large deep eyes had lost their lustre, her clear creamy skin looked dull and opaque. Even the magnificent hair seemed to have been robbed of its sheen, and here and there amidst its masses gleamed a silvery thread.

Up to this moment her age had been a matter of much speculation, varying from eighteen to twenty-six. Now one would have said unhesitatingly that she was a woman of at least thirty years, and a woman who did not carry those years lightly.

She sat down by Mrs. Jefferson, and spoke in a low nervous voice. "I knew I should find you here," she said. "I want your help. I think you have always been my friend here. Do me one service. Tell me what occurred in my room last night."

"Do you mean to say?" asked Mrs. Jefferson, amazed, "that you don't know?"

"Should I ask if I did?" she said, mournfully. "A great weight and terror are on my soul—yet I cannot explain them. In some of my trances I keep the memory of all I see; in some I lose it. I know nothing of what I said last night after you spoke and I parted from Julian. It was your voice that came between us. You have great psychic power; but it is undeveloped."

"Good gracious!" cried Mrs. Jefferson, "Then, if I'm responsible for what happened last night, I'll have nothing more to do with Occultism as long as I live."

"I can't tell why it was," resumed the Princess, mournfully. "The chain of communication broke, and I got away, and my great dread was that Julian should suffer."

"Well, your dread is realized," said Mrs. Jefferson. "Don't you know he's very ill?"

She started, and grew deadly white. "Ill—Julian! No; I did not know. What is it? —serious do they say?

"Very. Some shock to the brain. You know he was far from strong. He was only home from India on sick leave."

The princess was silent for a moment. Her

face looked inexpressibly mournful. Involuntarily her hand went to her heart, and she looked at Mrs. Jefferson with sad, appealing eyes. "I have suffered a great deal," she said, slowly. "I only bore it for his sake—for the hope they gave me that one day we should meet, and love, and taste the happiness of life together. Tell me, was it anything I said or revealed that shocked him?"

"Well—I guess so," said the little American, uneasily. "Of course, to us it was all mysterious; but he seemed to make it out, and at last, when you rose up and stretched out your arm and cried out, 'Die! in your crimes—*die!*' the Colonel just gave a sort of gasp, and crash went his chair, and he lay there on the floor like a dead creature. We were all finely scared, I can tell you. The odd part was that you went to sleep again like a child, just as simply and quietly as possible, and my husband and the poet, and poor old Diogenes, they got the Colonel to his room, and laid him on the bed, and we sent for a doctor, and he's not conscious yet. That's all I can tell you."

The Princess Zairoff leant back on her chair white and silent. She asked no more questions.

Presently an attendant appeared with obsequious inquiries. The princess suddenly shivered. "Ask them," she said, abruptly, "to bring up the temperature to 300°, I am cold."

"Cold!" Mrs. Jefferson stared. "I guess it's as well I came here first," she said, "for certainly I can't stand it 50° hotter than it is at present. I'll go into the second room. You see I'm reversing the usual order this morning. Three, two, one, instead of one, two, three. I'll sit just here by the door, so that we can still talk if you wish. I look like a boiled lobster, I'm sure."

Princess Zairoff said nothing. But when the American had withdrawn, she threw herself down on a couch near the wall. By choosing it she was out of sight of anyone in the adjoining room, though able to converse if she wished.

That she did not wish was very evident. No sooner was she alone than an expression of intense anguish came over her face. Her hands locked themselves together, an agony far beyond the weakness of tears was in her beautiful eyes.

" I have lost him," she cried, in a stifled whisper. "Lost him for ever . . . . and it was for this we were brought together . . . For this I was commanded to learn the secret of my failure. Yes, I, who thought myself so wise, have failed . . . Failed at the crucial test, because my passions governed me . . . because my heart was weak, for sake of love . . . Oh, my lost strength—my lost self-restraint . . . . Must I again tread the weary road . . . and only overcome to fail again?"

She turned aside and hid her face in her hands, while all that dusky veil of rippling hair fell over her like a cloud.

" I am so human still," she moaned—" so human that, woman-like, I deceived myself, and dreamt of love perfected here, when I might have known . . . I might have known . . . But, oh, to lose him thus ! To stand

before his eyes shamed, sin-stricken, criminal
. . . I cannot bear that . . . it is beyond
my strength . . ."

A new fierce passion seemed suddenly to
take possession of her soul. She raised herself once more, and the old lovely light and
splendour glowed in her eyes.

" There is but one way to win his for-
giveness," she cried breathlessly. " He will
pity me then . . . his heart will soften . . .
he will remember what I said on that strange
happy night when once again we met . . .
' I am but a woman who loves. Earth
holds no weaker thing ' . . . and I loved
you, Julian . . . you only—you alone !
always—always—always. Men live for love
—a woman can but die. For the life I took
I give my own . . . it is just . . . Yet if
but once, oh, beloved, I could see your pity-
ing eyes, and hear your tender voice . . . and
know that you—forgave . . . ."

The light faded from her face once more.
Only a hunted, despairing creature leaned
back on that solitary couch.

A voice came shrilly from the outer room :
" Are you all right, Princess ? Can you really
bear that heat ? "

Monotonously—vaguely—her own voice
replied : " I am all right . . . I do not even
feel the heat."

Then, all again grew still, and her eyes closed,
and her heart beat in a dull, laboured way.

Once more the shrill voice reached her ;
but it sounded far off, and indistinct : " I hope
you won't go off to sleep, like you did the last
time, Princess ; you frightened me terribly."

The effort to reply was harder to make; yet once again the slow, sweet voice vibrated through the hushed and stifling heat :

"I shall not sleep . . . do not be alarmed."

* * * * *

Five minutes later, when Mrs. Ray Jefferson lifted her eyes from an examination of her suffering foot, she was surprised to see the Princess standing in the archway of the further room, exactly as she had done on the first occasion of her visiting the Baths.

"Are you going ?" she called out. "How is it I never saw you pass through the room ?"

There was no answer—only the deep, wonderful eyes looked mournfully back at her, and, even as she met the gaze, the form seemed to fade away—the archway was vacant.

With a faint cry, Mrs. Jefferson sprang to her feet, and rushed into the inner room. The intense heat stifled, and drove her back; but not before she saw the Princess lying on the couch, where she had left her . . . lying with closed eyes and folded hands; while on her pale, sad lips a faint smile seemed still to shed its lingering life.

The frantic calls of the terrified woman summoned the attendants. In a moment, that motionless figure was lifted and carried into the adjoining chamber.

* * * * *

But human science and human aid were powerless before a greater Mystery than the Princess Zairoff had embodied. The "Mystery of Death!"

THE END.